Borderline Freaks MC #4

MariaLisa deMora

Edited by Hot Tree Editing

Proofreading by Whiskey Jack Editing

First Published 2019

ISBN 13: 978-1-946738-49-3

DEDICATION

As we express our gratitude, we must never forget that the highest appreciation is not to utter words, but to live by them. ~ President John F. Kennedy

Legacy is the evolution of legend.
To those who come along and take up
the reins to reign – Thank you.

Contents

ACKNOWLEDGMENTS

To know whether one is treading the straight and narrow depends entirely upon one's point of view.

Outlaws make their way through the world holding tight to only a few tenets. Revenge is one of them. Eye for an eye. Sometimes, however, there is a greater sense of justice when that payback is delayed.

That's the situation in which our good friends in the BFMC find themselves, trapped between man's law, and the rule of vengeance. The rhythm to which they sway reminds me of an old country tune, one that reminded boot-stomping dancers to take only a little, and give just a little more, ensuring it all comes right in the end. Balanced on the knife's edge to find a true path.

Thanks to you, the readers, for supporting this series and voting with your wallets. It's been written in a unique fashion for me, with the stories very nearly running end-to-end as the characters tell their tales.

If you've enjoyed it only half as much as I loved putting their words to the page, I'll count it a worthy effort.

Woofully yours,

~ML

See You in Valhalla

This is Angelo Dobbs' worst nightmare. A good man lies dead, and with the Borderline Freaks MC's president and founding member gone, the leadership position within the club falls to him.

It's not that he can't manage the easy task of leading a group of good men; he would just have preferred to stay a little farther out of the spotlight. But when his brothers issue the call, he answers.

Carly Gibson, daughter of his dead friend, is an unexpected—but not unwelcome—complication for his new role. She's the most intriguing woman he's ever met, capable and filled with a strength of character. He finds himself instinctively drawn to her. Could he have found the woman meant to complete him, finally?

Over the past couple of years, Dobbs—Neptune to the men of the BFMC—has watched as his closest friends found their soulmates. Now, their women are an integral part of the club. When they and Carly are threatened, Neptune will do anything to ensure their safety—and, just maybe, his future.

One

Neptune

"Gibby was a hell of a man."

Angelo Dobbs raised his glass in response to the shouted words, understanding to his core what the speaker meant. "Hear, hear!" His was one of a dozen voices lifted in response. A sea of hands held up drinks, and each of those hands tipped their containers, spilling a small amount on the floor before taking their own measure.

It had been two days since the club had laid their president in his grave. Matthew Gibson, affectionately known as Gibby, had been murdered nearly two weeks earlier. His body had been held for an autopsy, then further retained as the authorities attempted to find his next of kin.

He had listed a daughter on his paperwork, but no other family. Without her consent, it had become a battle, but the state police had finally authorized the release of his body to Angelo after he'd presented a document stating he was Gibby's executor. That was a full-on lie, but the forgery was one of the best Angelo could buy, and it had held up to the scrutiny of the staties as well as the coroner's office.

"Neptune." The utterance of his club name preceded the weight of a hand on his shoulder by only a fraction of a second, but it was enough to keep him from reacting negatively. "When are we voting?"

"How the fuck am I supposed to know?" Head angled, he scowled at the man standing next to him. "Monk, brother, you're as likely as I am to decide when we do whatever."

Monk was also an officer in the Borderline Freaks MC, his role the road captain. Neptune's was sergeant at arms, and their duties were different, but he'd never felt his was more important.

"Well, you know for sure it won't be Frootloop. He's fuckin' smashed, man." They both glanced over at their vice president, and Neptune saw Monk's headshake mirrored his own. "Word I heard is he's scared shitless he's gonna be tapped. You and me know better." Frootloop had gotten his officer plate from Gibby, whom he'd served under in the military. "I don't want it. Can't take it. Not with what I got goin' on. Blade's in no position to pick up the mantle, either, and we both know it. That leaves a small field, brother."

"Still, there's more options than just me." Neptune's skin itched with a need to move, a feeling he squashed ruthlessly, forcing his feet to stay in place as if cemented to the floor. "And I do not fuckin' want it."

"You'd be our best bet, and that's not me sayin' it'd be settlin' at all, brother. We'll be blessed with your hand at the helm. You were a leader in the corps, and you're a leader here in the BFMC." Monk's fingers dug into his shoulder, then lifted and clapped him in the center of his back. With his hand pressed tight to the patch Neptune wore, Monk said something that sounded way too much like an oath. "I'd follow you into hell and beyond, brother. 'Til Valhalla."

"Hope like fuck you don't have to." Neptune shook his head, gaze narrowed on Monk's face. He didn't see anything other than a genuine brotherhood there. Not that he'd expected to find deceit hiding amongst the well-known features, but old habits died hard. "I don't fuckin' want it, but if it's the will of the club, I'll do what's demanded."

"In that case." The weight of Monk's hand disappeared, and he lifted two fingers to his mouth. A whistle split the air. "Time to vote, brothers. No one can ever take Gibby's place, but we cannot be without a leader. With that said, I nominate Neptune." His initial shout quieted the crowd, but as silence fell around them, Monk's voice gained emotion, ragged pain at the grief forced upon them all.

Neptune had been played.

"Fucking hell."

"Seconded." Neptune turned to see Wolf standing along the wall to his other side. His friend shot him a somber smile and asked, "Mr. Secretary, are there other nominations?"

In response, Wheels, their secretary, held up a hand with five digits spread, slowly and silently tucking them into his palm as he counted down. When he had a fist without any additional names shouted, he called back to Wolf, "No, sir. No other members or officers put forth for consideration. All in favor?" He stuck his fist out, lifting it high. "So vote, now."

Every man raised a hand, fist pointing to the ceiling. All but Neptune. Teeth clenched, he held his peace, waiting for the process to come to an end. There was a reason parliamentary procedure was followed in tight or loose format, depending on the need. It was easily understood, provided a framework within which the men were held to clear expectations. Right now, they were voting for their club's leadership, selecting a man to sit at the head of the table. One who would set his stamp on the direction of the organization for the next few months, at least. Years, if Neptune allowed it to rock on that long.

"Mr. Secretary, do we have consensus?" Monk's question was clear, his tone triumphant as he turned to look at Neptune.

"We do, Road Captain. The nomination was seconded and voted, and there is no opposition." There was a brutal finality in Wheels' next words. "Neptune is president."

Neptune stared at Monk for another moment, then swept the room with his gaze, marking the expression on each face. Relief was most frequently represented, but pride existed, as did a subdued anticipation. He didn't see anything he didn't want, and that eased the tension in his gut. There was no anger or fear, and above all, no regret. *It's well and truly done.*

"My brothers—" He paused for effect, lifting his chin and stretching out the silence before he finished in the strongest voice he could muster. "I accept." Neptune raised his beer amidst the shouts and laughter, then led them in another acknowledgment, this one to cover their remaining guilt at moving on, calling out, "To Gibby."

"To Gibby." Every man drank deeply, any unease at the vacuum left after Gibby's death fading rapidly.

Neptune glanced across the room to where the gavel rested on a shelf that also held the lockbox with the club's charter papers. It had always bothered him that the important documentation was displayed like that, even if he'd understood why Gibby preferred it to be so. *Item one on the list of changes.* He snorted quietly at his own hubris in assuming he'd be making many of those decisions.

Monk blew out a heavy breath that he echoed, knowing it carried both regret and acceptance. Monk said, "Sloth'll give you the pres patch tomorrow. I had him have one made up, but I thought it could wait until after the wake's over."

They'd buried Gibby in his cut, founder patch still in place along with his officer plate. It hadn't been on him when he died, but they'd found it in his home, marking that as the place from which the murderers had taken him.

Now that his goal had been achieved, Monk stepped closer, voice lowered so it didn't carry. "You hear anything about that kid Gibby supposedly had?"

"Not a word. Putnam said he couldn't find evidence a Carly Gibson existed, at least not in conjunction with our Gibby." For a major of the local state troopers, Putnam wasn't a half-bad guy. Reasonable, even. "I gave him a list of base assignments and told him I'd let him know if I find anything going through Gibby's stuff."

The man's home had been willed to the club, and after the police had finished processing it as a scene of interest, Neptune, Monk, Wolf, and Blade had all started the tasks of sorting out personal from club with everything inside. It was a daunting responsibility. Gibby had lived in the same house for two decades, and alongside the normal detritus of a life well lived were various artifacts from the first days of the club.

Neptune looked around the room, noting the bevy of eyes still fixed on him. *Dammit.*

From here on out, that's what it would be, at least until he could give up the gavel he hadn't yet wielded. Center of attention, exactly where he never wanted to be. The area between his shoulder blades itched, an uncomfortable crawling sensation taking up residence just underneath the skin.

"What say we start planning a couple of things." He crooked a finger at Wolf and got a nod in response as his friend pushed off the wall he'd still been leaning on. A glance at Frootloop showed the man's clear relief at not being asked to take on the office but also proved he wouldn't be much help for anything today as he upended another beer, finishing the bottle fast. "Blade." Pitched low, Neptune's voice carried just far enough, and he saw his other friend turn and start walking his direction.

Once the three men were lined up in a semicircle facing him, Neptune blew out a quick breath. "We need a memorial ride, but it has to be organized with the other chapters in the area. The vote tonight has to be ratified by Mother, but I don't know of any reason they'd table it, which means your maneuvering bought you someone in this seat who isn't afraid to leverage all the assets at his disposal." He leveled a finger and dragged it in an arc, pointing at all of them in turn. "You, my brothers, are those assets."

"Seriously? It's been what?" Monk pretended to consult a watch on the bare back of his wrist. "Two minutes? You can't just stand still and *be* for two minutes?"

"Brother, you knew me before you tossed me into the deep end here. You ever known me to just be?" He lifted his top lip in a pretend sneer. "It's like you don't even know me." He *tsk*ed on the slow inhale before blowing out a deep sigh. "I'm offended."

"Put on. All of it's a put-on farce. Little liar." Blade offered the mild insult on a grin that slowly faded. Neptune felt the weight of his gaze for a minute, then Blade dipped his head deeply, lifting a fist to pound against Neptune's chest. "Prez." As if in slow motion, he watched as Monk and Wolf did the same, their voices filled with gravel. "Prez."

The import of their actions hit him all at once, and it took everything inside him to stifle the grief that welled up, suffocating him with a wave of darkness. Gibby was gone forever, killed at the hands of men denied their brotherhood. Men who'd proven unfit, not worthy. Gibby, along with the rest of the members, had made sure those men would never be members of not only the BFMC but of any respected club in a four-state area. In retribution, Gibby had been strung up in a tree, hanging there like trash waiting for a storm to come along and knock it down. It didn't matter who the men were, who they thought they had on their side. Their treatment of Gibby couldn't stand. Neptune wouldn't allow it.

The club had been waiting two weeks.

Holding their breath and waiting patiently to get Gibby back and give him the send-off he deserved.

"Brothers." Neptune reached out and gave them a salute similar to the one they'd offered him, thudding his fist firmly on each man's shoulder. Raising his voice, he called out to the members in the room, getting the attention of every man. "It's time."

Two

Carly

Her brain stuttered upon waking, trying to convince her body that it didn't hurt quite as badly as she knew it must. The rough, thin mattress under her cheek stank. It was grimy to the touch as she pushed upright into a sitting position, legs crisscrossed in front of her. Carly cleared her throat, wincing when a stinging burn rippled, following the sound, fading as she forced another burst of air through. Eyes opened to slits, she hung her head, hair in uneven hanks around her face to hide her from casual observers.

There were three of them today. That was fitting, since today marked three months since she'd been taken. Men in chairs pulled right up to the edge of the bars separating her from the hallway that led to outside and freedom. The armchairs were plush, which meant they'd been settled in for the long haul. No hard folding chairs for this bunch.

She shifted, and the metal cot under her swayed slightly, the chains holding it up rattling in their bolted holes. At first the movement had been hard for her to get accustomed to, the sickening way it swayed underneath her at the slightest provocation. Or slammed around violently when under great duress. Now it was just business as usual. *A body can get used to a lot of things.*

Licking her lips provided no relief from the parched dryness, and Carly worked her tongue along the insides of her teeth, having no luck in trying to stir up the least bit of saliva to swallow. *At least I won't need to pee anytime soon.* Or anything else. Only a few weeks into her captivity she'd tried to gross out the men who'd paid for their chance with her, bare ass hovering over the narrow-slit toilet as she'd strained. Turned out one of them had a scat kink. She shuddered at the memory. *Live and learn.*

Scratching at an insect bite on her arm with one thumbnail, she studied the faces of these men.

Uniformly Caucasian, uniformly wealthy appearance of entitlement, and uniformly painted with the asshole brush. The one in the middle wouldn't meet her eyes, and she decided he'd be her fainting goat today. Only one of the three would be allowed into the cage at the end of this extended prologue.

If she could force the encounter to work out as she wanted, she'd have a few minutes of peace. The losers didn't typically stick around to watch, and the guards wouldn't come traipsing by as long as the visitor was present. Privacy—not for her, but for the victor. The chosen one was smaller than the other two and pudgy in the middle, and had a timid appearance. Not a typical top-dog-looking guy, but she had confidence she could get him in, get him hard, and then choke him into ecstasy, repeating the process for as long as he'd last.

Ignoring the two men on either side of him, she kept her eyes on the mark, giving him tiny smiles when he'd lift his eyes to her face. She tried and failed a dozen times to snag his gaze, her attention so blatant the other two men had started shifting uncomfortably. Finally, he glanced up and she had contact, widening her eyes in feigned surprise as she turned her chin coquettishly to the side. It worked, as she'd known it would, and he'd gone from not looking at her to staring at her face. Carly licked her lips, watching as sweat sprang forth on his brow at the action. The sleeveless top she wore was loose, and she hooked a thumb in the arm, dragging it to the side and giving him a flash of boob that made his face redden, lips parting in a quick pant.

Rules in place said he had to ask and she had to accept. A two-way street, according to her faceless captor. And wasn't that a kick in the ass, being made to be party to her own rape. Her plans hadn't always worked out, and more often than she wanted to remember, she'd been overpowered, thrown on the cot, and taken. She'd trained for this, though, and been briefed that it was a known possibility when she'd accepted the job. It was just that deep down inside she hadn't expected it, hadn't thought it could really happen, just a one in a million chance that seemed worth the risk at the time. Each op before this one had ended the way she'd expected, but the closer she came to the main target, the chancier the opportunities became. She'd lost the roll of the dice this time. *Bad odds.* She shoved that thought into a box and lost it in a corner of her mind.

Focus back on her mark, she batted her eyelashes, face turned far enough towards him that he could see her smile. *Sell it*, she thought. *Make him think you want it.* His mouth opened, and she was already gearing up to agree when their forced transaction was interrupted by a racket from up the hallway. She heard muffled shouts in at least three languages, and doors slammed, the loud reverberation of metal impacting against stone walls rolling through the air and shivering through the cot underneath her.

Nerves prickled throughout her body, and she whirled to stare past the bars, as far up the hallway as her position allowed. The men in the chairs had all turned in the same direction, their faces going pasty white, and she noticed something she hadn't seen before. Each of them bore a mark on his wrist, a black slash across the thin skin. She'd seen the same marks before, but not on men. It had been branded into the upper arms of children rescued from a sex farm.

Finally. In her mind, the connection she'd been looking to make for six long months came clear.

The air turned heavy and then left in a whoosh, traveling up the hallway towards the disturbance.

Carly threw herself from the cot, leaving it clanking and swaying behind her as she scrambled into the corner of the cell, dragging the scant protection of the mattress behind her.

The air caught fire a few moments after she'd huddled in on herself, arms holding the mattress around herself protectively as she pushed into the angle created by two walls.

The flashover only lasted a few seconds, still long enough to have the fabric on her back nearly hot enough to smolder, the exposed skin on her body stinging. Echoing effects of what she assumed was a blast were deafening, and when she turned and pushed the mattress out of the way to look at the hallway, she saw the stark results. The three men were still upright in their chairs, clothing burned away and exposing the restraints she hadn't realized were holding them to the flaming chairs. Their mouths were open in screams, long, thin warbles of sound that dug into her ears, setting up a resonance in her head she knew she'd never completely get rid of.

A man stepped into view, hulking shoulders eclipsing the light coming from behind him. He eased around the men and grabbed the door of her cell, giving it a hard shake even as he hissed in pain. Pulling back, he lifted a massive boot and kicked twice, the hinges of the door giving way finally.

Carly licked her lips and stood staring at the opening for only a minute. She turned her gaze to the man and lifted her chin in response to his similar movement, then tried on a grin that felt much too small for her lips. "All this, for me?"

"Get over here." His gruff demand caused a hot burning at the backs of her eyes, and Carly slowly slid her lids closed as she blindly walked into his arms. His mouth was beside her ear a moment later, and over the dwindling screams of the dying men, she heard him say brokenly, "Sister, I'm sorry."

"Nope." Fingers clutching at the back of his shirt, she shook her head, rough fabric dragging in the tears streaming down her cheeks. She knew what he was going to say, because it was the same guilt she'd have carried if it were him lost and locked up in a place like this. He'd be feeling responsible, and she needed to nip this in the bud before he tried to take on more than what was truly his. "You found me. That's all that matters."

"*Carly.*" The single word carried so much pain, and she hated to hear it.

"Ryman, I'm alive. Everything else is recoverable." She shuffled backwards a step and peered up into his face, noting the new lines etched into his features. Gaunter than the last time she'd seen him; his hair and beard were unkempt. She knew it was because he'd spent all his time between then and now looking for her. There was a raised ridge of tissue that ran under one ear and down the back of his neck. Her lungs clenched at the sight of the red, angry, and very new scar. *He didn't have that three months ago.* During her abduction had been the last time she'd seen Ryman. For twelve long weeks, her recurring dreams had reminded her every night that she'd been taken as he lay crumpled on the floor, his head covered by a wash of red. *He got that protecting me.* "Got anything for me?"

He stared at her for a long moment as the sounds of fighting in the distance diminished and ended. Whatever he'd seen in her face had been enough, because he nodded and shrugged out of a backpack, slinging it across his chest to access the compartments. In short order, he handed her a Glock, then a rig for her shoulder along with a Sig Sauer, and finally a bundle of fabric wrapped around something heavy. She backed to the cot and looked down, then gestured towards him with a flip of one hand.

"Got a camera?" He nodded and hesitated before he took a step inside, leaning back almost immediately and looking up the hallway. He waved once, which she took to mean his guys had won, then stalked towards her, pulling out a phone. She pointed to the flat metal surface exposed when she'd moved the mattress. He aimed the device and triggered it, the blinding flash startling her as it revealed the scratches in the paint and metal. Names and dates, and cryptic letters describing the details around why she'd recorded the information. "It's him, and this proves it. It's him, Ryman. With the marks on those men's arms, this is everything we need."

"Jesus, Carly." He grabbed the metal cot and held it still, moving to take more pictures of the additional information.

She stripped efficiently, dragging the clean clothing over her body. She'd hoped to hide the still-healing wound from Ryman but knew she'd been unsuccessful when he cursed lowly, the sound harsh in the quiet surrounding them. Without looking over her shoulder, she told him, "Knife, nearly a month ago. I'm okay, Ryman." She used the ragged clothing she'd discarded to wipe her feet, standing on top of the boots he'd provided to pull on the thick socks, then the boots themselves. The holster rig was last, and she shrugged into it, rolling her shoulders a couple of times to settle it into place before tightening the straps. Glock in hand, she took a final look around the cell, this twelve-by-sixteen room that had been her entire world for far too long. Suddenly, the few minutes that had passed since Ryman kicked in the door seemed an eternity, and she was overwhelmed with the need to get out, get away. "Ready?" Her voice wasn't steady, but fortunately Ryman ignored that telling quaver, answering her with a grunt as he moved ahead of her towards the hallway.

"You're alive." She didn't know if he'd intended the words as positive reinforcement or a promise, but she took them at face value, a reassurance her partner of three years needed to get past the knowledge that she'd been abducted and he'd been left behind for dead.

She hadn't been able to save him, either.

"We both are."

Three

Neptune

"Hold on, hold on." Laughter interspersed with the words, light and free. "Hold on, dammit." More laughter, and on the TV screen, the group of men clustered in a group paused, lofting the chair with the man installed like a throne. "Put me down already."

"No way." Shouted agreement with the denial was also liberally sprinkled through with laughter. "You're in the king seat, brother."

"All right then, if you're gonna do this thing, do it up right."

Neptune watched the face of the man in the cheap plastic lawn chair, smiling as Gibby made a show of lifting his arms, proving trust of the men holding him high. Like a little kid at an amusement park, he danced his hands through the air, swooping side to side as the chair moved, just as if he were in the front seat of a roller coaster. Hair blowing into his face, Gibby shouted for a beer—and when it came in an underhand toss, caught it easily. The top popped with a loud hiss, froth bubbling out and over the men below him.

Through the shouted insults and laughter, Gibby's voice was clear as he called out, "Fuck, I shoulda shook it. Christened all your asses."

Neptune paused the video there and stared at the screen.

Wide smile stretching from ear to ear, Gibby looked as easy and relaxed as if he'd been floating down the river in an innertube. Nothing about his face said he was poised for a crash six feet above the ground. There was no stress, no strain, and no fear on his features. There was only trust. A deep and abiding trust in his men, his *brothers*, the members of the club he'd chartered.

Neptune hung his head and stared at his hands clasped between his knees, remote wedged between his palms. It was a week after the wake, and he was back in Gibby's house, sorting through what remained. Which was proving to be a lot.

The club had come together the previous few days, finishing with the Borderline Freaks portion of the things

Gibby'd left behind. Those artifacts were all gone, cleared out, in storage at the clubhouse waiting for an appropriate way to display the founder's roots that had given their club life.

Now it was just Gibby's personal items, and Neptune had taken it on, turning away all offers of assistance, needing this chance to say goodbye to the best friend he'd ever had. He'd known Gibby for years and loved him like a brother through all of those.

Until half an hour ago, he'd have said he and Gibby knew each other inside and out, stem to stern and back again. The video he'd been watching had been one of a dozen on a thumb drive Neptune had found on Gibby's nightstand. They were all from club events.

He glanced down at a book on the coffee table in front of him, then back up at the screen, trying to reconcile the man he'd known with the one depicted in the images bound inside that book.

One was the free and easy biker, club president and mentor, driving force behind all things BFMC.

The other was a starry-eyed newlywed, doting father, and complete stranger to Neptune.

Hidden in a box within a box underneath Gibby's bed, the photo album had been buried underneath layer after layer of loose images. Pictures of the club, faces growing younger with each exposed layer, until he'd found an image of Gibby without a vest. There was a hearse in the background, a tent in the grass with lines of chairs underneath, and row after row of granite stretching off into the distance.

In the foreground of the picture was Gibby. Palm resting on the handlebars of a bike, he was straddling the seat. This version of the not-yet-old Gibby was staring straight at the camera, a girl of maybe fourteen balanced in front of him. He looked stricken, but the agony plain on his face held nothing on the little girl's. She looked enough like Gibby to make the connection easy, even with her red-rimmed eyes that spoke of deep pain. On the back of the picture was a date and one word: Carly.

Inside the photo album was a linear record of Gibby's life before the club. High school graduation, prom king with an arm slung around a girl who'd appeared in a multitude of other images in those pages. The pretty girl from prom was even more gorgeous dressed all in white, lilies held low in front of her swelling baby bump. Basic training, first deployments, rotations home for leave. Neptune's throat closed as he looked at Gibby's face in profile, eyes closed as his lips pressed gently against the sweet curve of a baby's head, pink bow in the background.

There were jumps in the timeline, the baby going from infant to her sixth birthday within a couple of pages, luminous blue eyes and a snaggle-toothed smile staring from across the top of a peppermint cake. The images skimmed her childhood, pool parties followed by awkward poses in formal dresses alongside hulking jocks. Then a picture of the girl, little no more, dark hair pinned in a severe bun that went perfectly with her fatigues, arm around Gibby.

Neptune clicked around on the laptop he'd connected to the TV until he found the file on the thumb drive he wanted. Not a video, but an audio recording; the timestamp was just over three years ago.

"Daddy." Crisp and clear, just that one word held affection enough for a lifetime. Neptune closed his eyes. "I've got a chance to make a difference. It's him, Daddy. I know it is. I can do this. I know you won't like it, but it's what I want to do. Remember that, okay? This is my choice. I'm going to be out of touch for a while." She paused, and her voice was huskier when she continued. "Probably for a long time. Don't look for me. I'll let you know when it's safe for me to be in contact again. It's... This is *my choice*." The emphasis on those last words wasn't lost on Neptune. Clearly Gibby would have lost his mind at whatever she'd been planning. "My handlers said they'd take care of telling you, but I know you, Daddy. You'd have come looking for me anyway. I can hear you now, telling me, 'Damn, Carly, you got some balls on you.' I can make a difference, Daddy. I have to do this. I'll be safe as I can be, I promise." Her voice wavered for the first time when she repeated herself. "I promise." There was another quiet pause, but the recording continued, so Neptune kept listening. "So this is for those birthdays and Christmases I might miss. Father's Day, too. Happy Christmairthday, Daddy. I love you." As with the previous times Neptune had listened, what followed was the hiss of dead air, then a click, and the recording ended.

Gibby had a daughter. Who, if the statement about her handlers was correct, had gone undercover on some kind of sting operation more than three years ago. Whatever it was had been serious enough that Gibby had erased any mark of her in his house. Neptune remembered the first time he'd come to his president's house for dinner and silently noted the empty places on the walls. He suspected those places had once been filled with some of the images he'd found inside the box.

Gibby had a daughter.

It struck him suddenly that he'd set the state police looking for her. Neptune found himself seized by an uncharacteristic hesitation, unsure in that instant if he should call Putnam and wave them off. He could have a quiet conversation and disclose what he'd found here today, but what if that only spurred the man onward? If he claimed to have found her himself, would that be enough to throw the man off the scent?

If whatever she was doing was dangerous enough that Gibby had wiped her from his life, never breathing a word about her, was it possible Neptune had put her into the very danger Gibby'd been trying to save her from?

He heard a rattling sound from the back of the house and made a mental note to plan on a prospects' day at Gibby's. He could set them to the task of trimming up the bushes and tree limbs and preparing the house to sit empty. Even if Gibby'd left it to the club, Neptune was damned if he knew what to do with it. He couldn't even think of selling it, not with all the memories every member had of this house and meals sitting at the same table as their president. Moments that mattered to the men, those of being seen by and having their company valued by a man they admired.

Glancing around, he realized it had grown dark as he'd sat here, night falling outside, stretching shadowy fingers into the room. Even the computer had gone to sleep, leaving both screens dark.

The rattle came again, sounding more metallic, a scrape and drag that had his hair standing up on end. Someone was trying to break in. Wouldn't be a BFMC member. They all knew where the extra key was, and Neptune was pretty sure he hadn't locked the front door anyway. Whoever this was, they were attempting a stealth entry at the rear of the building, and the anger bubbling inside him ensured he'd be foiling whatever plans they had.

Not on my watch.

Soft-footing it up the hallway, he paused in the doorway leading into the kitchen to listen, rewarded by a hushed indrawn breath from the mudroom. It was followed by a stealthy click of the door seating into the latch. *They're inside.* A darker shadow crept along the floor, stretching halfway across the room. He held still and watched; something about that shadow was disquieting in a way he didn't understand. It lengthened and thinned the farther the form got from the window allowing the moonlight, and it felt somehow frail to him.

A figure appeared in the doorway and stepped through. Shorter than he'd expected; their shoulders seemed narrower than they should have been. Then, something in the way they moved told him the truth. *A woman.*

Chin up, he took a step into the room and clipped a curt, "Hey."

She whirled to face him, fine features exposed for only an instant in the uncertain light, yet he still recognized her. Red-rimmed lids held the same luminous blue eyes she'd shared with her father.

"Carly." She stiffened when he said her name but didn't deny it, instead retorting with an angry-sounding curse.

"Why are you in my father's house?" Her demand was brittle, shards of pain laced through the broken sounds. "Who are you?"

"Hey, I'm a friend of your dad's." Neptune swept the wall with his hand, finally connecting with the switch for the overhead fixture, flooding the room with light and pushing back the shadows. "I'm a friend."

"I don't have any friends here." She was blinking in the sudden brightness, pale cheeks showing the shining tracks of recent tears. "Just my dad."

"You're Carly, right?" Her chin lifted as her shoulders arched back, stance forming an almost perfect parade rest that spoke volumes to her continued involvement with the military. "Gibby's little girl?" *Fuck, does she even know?*

His fears were put to rest with her next question. "You know...knew my dad?"

Neptune nodded, taking another step into the room, holding one hand down low. He touched his chest with his other. "Yeah, he was my best friend. Carly, I... We tried to get in touch with you."

"So I heard." She shuffled back a step and put her hip against the edge of the counter. "Until two days ago I was unreachable." Her neck sagged, head hanging low, hair in a tumble around her face. "I came as soon as I was notified."

Another noise from the mudroom door had him stepping forwards to put himself between her and whatever was coming.

Carly laughed, the sound dark and wrong. "That'll be my shadow. He'll be wanting to know who you are, and you'll be asking the same, I expect."

A man stomped through the doorway. He ignored Neptune, even though they were evenly matched physically. His anger-filled eyes were locked on the woman. "Would it have killed you to wait a half a fucking second, Carly? I was right behind you." Neptune sidestepped in front of him to cut off his approach, and the man's gaze finally swung to him. "And who the fuck are you?"

"I'm the asshole who's standing here asking you the same thing." Neptune kept his tone even, conversational, but he didn't pull the punch of his fist meeting the man's chest and holding him at bay. Not hard enough to break anything, but more than enough to sting. "Her I know from her baby pictures." It didn't hurt to exaggerate a little bit, giving the impression he actually knew Carly. "You, I don't know at all. Who are you and why are you here?"

When the man unfolded the final couple of inches, Neptune saw he'd been right about them being matched. Gaze flicking between a now-silent Carly and Neptune, the man shook his head. "Carly invited me."

An unfeminine snort came from behind Neptune, and he let his lips curl the slightest amount. "Did she now? Sounds to me like you followed her instead of being invited. Should I ask her?"

"Jesus, stop posturing already. Y'all are exhausting me." Carly brushed past Neptune, her body contacting all along his side even though there was ample room for her to have moved by without touching. He wasn't complaining, far from it. Just that touch from her was enough to have his nerves singing. It was a distraction he didn't need, however. "Ryman, this is my dad's best friend. Best friend, this is my partner and handler, Ryman."

"Best friend have a name?" Ryman backed up a step, not to get away from Neptune's reach but to avoid Carly as she stalked towards the refrigerator.

"Dobbs." Providing only his government name until trust was earned was always how Neptune went. He knew it was a moot point here, because his nameplate was on his chest, bold as brass, right under the officer patch proclaiming him president.

Carly proved herself observant when she half turned, refrigerator door partially open, and stared at him. "Neptune," she commented, and he nodded. "Why does that suit you so well?" That was a musing tone, and when he didn't respond, she shook her head and dipped to look into the cool interior of the fridge. The club's old ladies had restocked yesterday, knowing he and other members would continue to spend time here.

Carly came back into view with a jug of milk in one hand, the other giving the door of the fridge the exact amount of push needed to close it gently, more proof she'd probably lived here with Gibby at some point. She unerringly found the glasses and poured herself some milk, then, jug in hand, upended the glass in a single, long drink. She poured herself another half glass of milk before setting the jug on the counter and turning to face him. "Do you know more than the cops?"

"About?" He knew what she was asking, but without more information about what she'd been doing and why she'd been gone from her father's life for so long, he couldn't see himself giving her anything of interest beyond what she would glean from the police reports.

She stared at him a moment, then swung her gaze to Ryman, who had retreated to lean against the mudroom doorframe. "Did you intercept what I got?" He shook his head, and she scoffed far back in her throat. Lifting one hand, she turned her face away and used her nails to scratch through her hair, working her way along one side of her scalp. Her mouth worked, opening and closing, tightening and lips pursing several times before she pulled in a long breath. "Okay." Her mouth worked again, jaw tensing as she clenched her teeth. "Okay." She turned and faced Ryman, and Neptune felt sidelined somehow, as if he weren't important enough for her attention, and he didn't like that. Not at all. "Fifteen days before you got me out, my father was murdered. He was found hanging from a tree only a couple of miles outside of town. A tip had been called in to his club, the Borderline Freaks, and they followed it, not knowing what it meant. That's it. That's all the cops claim to know." She paused, and Ryman's attention left her for an instant; the glare directed Neptune's way said his role wasn't appreciated. "Hey." At her rough call, Ryman reengaged, his gaze directed back to Carly. "That give you enough to go on?"

"Yeah, sister." Without another word, Ryman turned and left, the door closing quietly behind him.

Carly's head dipped, and she pulled in another hard breath, and another, then one that broke in the middle. Her shoulders shook, and he took a quick step forwards, intending to support her somehow, but at his movement, she darted away, already steps out of reach before he could reach her. Back pressed to the front of the refrigerator, she stared at the floor next to his boots, only giving him sidelong glances as she tried and failed to reassure him. "I'm okay."

"I'm not." Before he could consider the potential cost of being honest with her, the words were out of his mouth. The wound in his chest, the pain that never went away, gaped a little more, releasing the sting of regret and anger deep inside him. "I fuckin' miss him."

Her head lifted, and she looked at him for so long Neptune became uncomfortable, her gaze hard and dark. Finally her lips parted, the tip of her pink tongue darting momentarily into view. In a voice soft but not tentative, she asked, "Did he suffer?"

Neptune straightened his shoulders, adopting the same pose she'd worn earlier. At attention, but ready to move at the slightest provocation. Parade rest, the same position he and the rest of the BFMC had held during Gibby's funeral. From the look on her face, Carly didn't want some mealy-mouthed version of what happened. Gaunt as she appeared, and given her admission that she was only days out from under whatever mission it was that had taken her from her father's life for so long, he still read into her expression that she wanted the truth.

"He fought until his final breath." From the blood on the tip of one boot, Neptune knew that even dangling from the hanging tree Gibby had fought viciously, kicking one of his attackers hard enough to mark. His knuckles had been split to the bone, proof of the way he'd fought. Even his nails and teeth had had flesh and blood embedded. One man against many, he'd employed every tactic possible. "He didn't go easy."

"I'd expect no less from the old man." Her tears had started afresh, but Neptune did his best to ignore them as she was doing. His fingers itched to wipe the tears from her cheeks, wanted to fold her in something soft and keep her safe. She cleared her throat and gritted out, "Hard-ass to the end."

"One of the best men I've ever had the privilege to know." Neptune folded his arms across his chest, uncertain what to do with this unrelenting need to comfort her somehow. "I was proud to call him friend and brother."

"Neptune, was it?" Lips pulled into a rictus of a smile, she tipped her head to the side as she waited.

"Dobbs." *I haven't given you that yet, doll*. Not sure why it annoyed him so much, Neptune narrowed his eyes as he glared at her audacity.

"Dobbs, then. Are you staying here tonight?" She made a noise far back in her throat as she moved back to where the milk container sat on the counter, busying herself with putting it away and rinsing her glass. She kept her face hidden, aiming the curved plane of her back to him. "Well?" She prompted him for an answer, and he held his tongue, waiting for her to turn and face him.

"No, I was planning on going home." There was a flash of something that crossed her face, there and gone so fast he nearly didn't see it. *Fear.* "I could stay if you wanted."

"I…" She cleared her throat, the sound raw in the silence stretching between them. Eyes glistening with unshed tears, she ducked her head and, as if it were a weakness to be ashamed of, admitted, "I'd like to hear more about Daddy, if you don't mind. I could use the company, too."

He stared at her a moment, then nodded slowly, finally giving a verbal affirmation when she didn't look up. "I can stay. I found some videos you might like to see."

"You've got stories, too? Daddy always said bikers made the best oral historians. When it's not safe to put anything to paper, stories are how the tales are told and remembered." She turned away again and fell silent. He watched as her shoulders rose and fell with slow, steady breaths as she leaned, her palms flattened on the counter. "I saw some beer in the fridge. Want one?"

The title Ryman had given her hadn't gone unnoticed by Neptune, and he employed it now, hoping she understood the kind of respect it granted in only a few syllables. "Love a beer, sister. And I've got stories for days about your daddy. Let's go in the living room, play a little show-and-tell."

Four

Carly

Sitting in her rental car, she stared through the window at the front door of the place her father had called his home away from home. Above the porch, directly between the upstairs windows, was an emblem that had been created with bold, black slashes of paint onto the wood, likely by her father's hands. Borderline Freaks MC. She knew she didn't have a place here and would probably be turned away, but she'd wanted to see.

She'd been aware of his biker friends growing up, but by the time he'd founded the club here in town, she'd been away at school. And of course over the past few years, she'd been undercover more than not, which meant there were whole sections of his life that were blanked out, incomprehensible to her. Now that he was gone, those secrets were unrecoverable, a profound loss she couldn't wrap her head around.

The door opened, and a man's body filled the opening, stepping out of the darkness but stopping short of the sunlight striking the porch at an afternoon angle. Half hidden by shadows as he was, she still recognized him. *Neptune.*

Even now, just the sight of him filled her with a melancholy mix of sadness and grief, followed closely by a dangerous tingle of faint lust. Dangerous because he was the antithesis of so many things she stood for. This was the very reason she and her father had fought more than once, because she'd known he wasn't always totally legal in what he did. There was no way that Dobbs—he'd made it clear she didn't have the right to call him by his club name—was any less an outlaw than her old man had been.

Carly let her breath out in a long, slow sigh, lifted a hand in goodbye, and put the car in reverse. She'd twisted in the seat to look over her shoulder, easing towards the street, when there was a rattling thump on the top of her car. Jamming the brakes on, she whirled to see Dobbs standing beside her door.

Heart pounding, she thumbed the control and lowered the window, heat rushing in to make sweat prickle along her skin. "Hey. Hi." She didn't try to hide her surprise at his actions. "I just wanted to look the place over for a minute. Didn't mean to bother anyone."

"And that's it?" Fists planted on each hip, he stared down at her, eyes narrowed in apparent annoyance. As she'd thought, her appearance here wasn't welcome.

"Yeah. I just wanted to see it." Fingers wound tightly around the wheel, she pressed harder on the brake pedal, needing an outlet for her nervous energy. "I didn't think anyone would notice me."

"We keep watch on all our places. Clocked you on security half a block away. Boys called me." Neptune leaned over, face thrust closer to hers. "And you didn't want to come in? Just a drive-by'll do for you?"

"Well, yeah, if it has to. Of course I'd love to see those pictures you were talking about last night." He'd talked for hours about her father, his respect and love for Gibby bleeding through with every word spoken. During the process, he'd talked about the memorial wall that had come together in the clubhouse, every member bringing a different view of the man to their offerings. "But I didn't expect I'd be welcome."

"Why?" He moved, hands now resting on the doorframe only inches from her. "You're Gibby's." He paused, and there was a weight in the silence. His voice had dropped to a growl when he finished with, "You're ours."

"Dobbs, we don't run in the same circles." That was as plain as she could state it without making a comment that might be construed as a threat, something she knew wouldn't be met with just disapproval but potential conflict, something she found herself wanting to avoid. "I'm not like Daddy was."

"You're more like him than you know, Carly." He straightened and took a step back, and she missed his closeness immediately. "Pull back up here and park. Come inside. My guest."

She waited for a reversal of the invitation, and when it didn't materialize, she nodded, then ducked her head as she shifted gears. "You're going to regret this later." Carly'd thought she'd kept her mutter quiet enough but knew he'd overheard her when he laughed, the sound booming. She looked up in time to catch the open-mouthed smile directed her way.

"Carly girl, I've made a lotta mistakes in my life, but I decided long ago that not a one of them was worth a moment's regret." He retreated another step and stopped, staring at her. "Park it. Come in with me."

Climbing out of the car, she ignored the outstretched hand and then pretended an extreme interest in the BFMC emblem on the front steps. Cunningly painted across just the bends between the steps and the kickboards, it was revealed only as a person approached that first step, but had been laid across the wood in such a way that it never took a footfall. She smiled as she realized the hidden meaning she knew her father had been behind. It put the club front and center as it should be but kept the members and guests from walking all over it. "Metaphors were one of his favorite things."

"Yeah," Neptune agreed from beside her. "He was always big on the symbolic reasoning behind many of the things we take for granted these days." He huffed out a soft chuckle. "Man could talk for days about the founding fathers and their intent as decoded by him."

"Oh, Lord." She laughed quietly. "Don't get him started on Lincoln's death. You'd be having breakfast before he slowed enough for another person to get a word in edgewise."

"Coulda used your insight a few years ago." Neptune opened the door, but instead of standing back to invite her in, he preceded her into the shadows. "House," he called loudly, and she heard the scuffing of chair legs against bare wood. "Brothers, Gibby's girl's here. Carly. His little girl's come for a visit."

Carly had stopped in her tracks at the beginning of his introduction, and she didn't move until his arm stretched back towards her, fingers gripping her hand to draw her through the opening. She noted about twenty men in scattered groups as she glanced around, scanning for threats, exits, agents, weapons...then shook herself. *This is Daddy's clubhouse, not a cartel holding pen in Colombia.* The men in the room were staring at her, a mix of expressions on their faces that she read as ranging from interest to anger, disdain, and all the way to boredom.

The tableau was broken by a tall man striding toward her, hand outstretched. "Monk," he offered, and she met his palm with her own. He used the grip to yank her close, wrapping an arm around her shoulders as her other hand planted on his chest, ready to shove away. She tensed as, with his mouth close to her ear, he muttered, "Sucks to meet you like this, but Gibby'd be glad you are here now." The pain in his voice fit against the edges of her own grief, and the emotions swelled inside her, rising to choke her to silence.

Without waiting for a response she didn't think she could muster anyway, he was gone, and another man stood in front of her, arms lifted to crush her to him with a savage pull. "He was a good man, a fucking good man. I'm Blade, honey child. Your daddy's gone on, but he'd be happy as fuck to see you here."

It went on like that for long minutes, the scuff of boot leather against the floor a buoy bell telling of the tide of men encircling her. Early on in the process, a hand had settled in the middle of her back, and she instinctively knew the support came from Neptune. She could compartmentalize with the best of them, finishing an op and putting it into a box in her mind, set aside to make room for the next, and the next. Here she didn't have the freedom to take her time. There was no debrief between the first wave and the following ones. These men had been drifting since her father's death, and now she'd provided a target for their grief. Neptune's firm touch held her in place against the more vigorous approaches, anchoring her against the swell of the emotional confessions, a welcome presence that told her in a tangible way that she wasn't alone. Even in the midst of these strangers who were laying claim to the broken bits of her heart, she wasn't alone.

Cheeks wet, she'd lost the ability to beat back the tears, walls around her heart crashing down with each of their muttered memories of her father, telling her truths according to the code they lived by. They spoke of his loyalty, the strength of his convictions, the wisdom he'd been happy to bestow on his brothers. How he worried about them all, chiding them into making better lives for themselves, convincing them they were worth the fight. *He was loved.* That was the thought circling her head, repeating in loud shouts and soft whispers. No matter how far she'd run or how long she'd had to stay away, he hadn't been alone after all. *He was so very loved.*

Each man who'd approached had done so exposing his emotions, the raw pain steadily scraping at her control. After one member had backed away, broken and crying at his own poignant recitation of grief, Carly covered her face with one hand, finding the fingers of her other one twined together with Neptune's. A steadying arm wrapped around her shoulders, and she was pulled into a close embrace. "Y'all give her just a minute, yeah?" His voice was low and rumbled through his chest where her ear was pressed tight to the hard wall of muscles. Nearer her ear, he murmured, "I got you, gal. You let go if you want to. I got you."

The hot tears flowed after that, soaking his shirt as he held her, rocking them back and forth in a comforting slow dance there in the middle of the clubhouse. His grip on her had renewed again and again, each shift in position telling her he was still there with her, right there in the middle of the rubble of her life, and she hadn't known she'd needed that until it was offered so damned freely. His words, a constant melodic croon in her ear, told her of his own grief and loss, that her father had been more than a leader, had been more than a friend—they'd been brothers to the bone, one voice between them as they'd worked to better the club.

Some of those secrets she'd feared lost forever had been revealed over the course of the past hour, and now she drank in these new memories given voice by this huge bear of a man. Her giggle at one of the stories startled both of them, and she pulled back, lifting her chin to stare up into Neptune's eyes, finding them red-rimmed. Stiffening her spine, she attempted to take a step backwards, but his arms tightened around her, restricting that retreat. "Dobbs—"

"Neptune." He cut her off with a word, and the permission granted with that one word fanned a tiny curl of heat in her belly. His palm cupped her jaw, and she felt the glide of his thumb across the curve of her cheek. "I know you're gettin' this, but I'll say it plain. Gibby mattered to us. All of us." His eyes lifted, breaking their stare as he glanced around the room over the top of her head before his gaze returned to hers. "We have a memorial ride for him this afternoon. I'd be honored if you'd ride on my bike, Carly. There's a bunch of guys coming in from other chapters and clubs, and it'll do us all good to see you there."

The idea of riding on a motorcycle behind this man tightened that curl of lust, wringing out every atom of desire she'd ever felt. Eyes locked with his, she studied him closely. He blinked, and his face changed, softening. She saw the sorrow she'd heard in his voice, but it was shadowed by heat, and she realized that for some unknown reason, he badly wanted this.

Throwing caution to the wind, she took in a deep breath that swelled her ribs, pressing her breasts against him. His arm gave her a squeeze. She felt a thickening at his groin and had to fight the urge to moan and arch into him more.

Ignoring all of that, she gave him the answer he wanted.

"I'd love to, Neptune."

LACK OF IN-BETWEEN

Five

Neptune

Bikes had been rolling in for the better part of an hour, and he stood with his shoulders pressed tight to the outside wall of the clubhouse, arms folded across his chest as he watched over the proceedings. Monk's old lady, Amanda, and Blade's woman, Jenn, were handling the registration, lines snaking away from where the women sat, piles of completed paperwork piling up between them. The men working the raffles and drawings were doing their jobs, and he saw another prospect swap in an empty jar for one filled with bills. The club had borne the cost of Gibby's headstone but knew the whole community would want to have a hand in some kind of memorial, so Monk had come up with the idea of a flagpole and flag near Gibby's grave. At this rate,

Neptune figured they'd have more than enough money to pay for that and more by the end of the day.

Another bike pulled up, this one alone, and he studied the unfamiliar rider. He swore when he finally recognized the man as the same one from Gibby's place yesterday. The one Carly had claimed as a partner and handler, the man who'd held her life in his hands while she'd been undercover. *Ryman.*

Neptune pushed off the wall and rattled down the steps, striding through the crowd without looking to either side. He came to a halt just a pace away from the big man still seated on the bike. He didn't wait for a greeting, just dove right to the heart of the matter without bothering to work through the why of his anger at this man's appearance. "The fuck you think you're doing here?"

"Paying my respects." Ryman stood and lifted a leg, swinging to stand on the other side of the bike, putting the machine between them. "Same as every other man here."

"Yeah, right." Ryman had on jeans and scuffed biker boots, a ragged and faded T-shirt covered with a blank denim vest that was worn in all the right places. He looked like a Hollywood extra, dressed for the part. *Shit had to have cost him a pretty penny on such short notice.* Neptune gestured towards the man, holding his gaze with a glare. "You think this is a joke, man? This your way of playing biker for a day?"

"I live in Picklewood." He named a community about forty miles east and south of town. "This here"—he patted the fuel tank on the bike—"is my girl, Shillelagh." He gestured to his front, indicating his clothes. "And these are what I wear when I ride her. Which isn't often enough, given the work I do." Ryman straightened and gave Neptune's glare back to him, multiplied. "When my partner told me about the ride, I dropped everything to be here. For her. Not to somehow spite you, asshole. You don't factor that much, so don't flatter yourself. This—" He gestured around them, then back to the bike between them. "Me being here, this is about Carly. Get over yourself."

Neptune's chin rose, and he gritted his teeth, muscles in his jaw complaining at the strain. "Apologies." He swallowed hard, then rolled his neck when he realized why the true reason the man being here was torquing him over. "I'll bring you the helmet I got for Carly."

He'd already turned away when the man's voice stopped his movement. "Dobbs?" Neptune looked over his shoulder to where Ryman stood, a puzzled look on his face. "She's not riding with me."

He turned back to face the man. "Why not?" Now he was unreasonably angry on Carly's behalf, thinking this man had tossed her aside without even an argument. "She not worth the effort?"

"Fuck, man." Ryman's head shook back and forth in short sweeps. "She's my partner, but we're not...the woman's gorgeous, sure, but she's got the wrong parts for me. She's excited about this, and I haven't heard that in her voice in a while. I know you don't have a clue what she's gone through in the past couple of years, but trust me when I say hearing her that way makes me fuckin' giddy for her. She doesn't even know I'm here, man. Right now, she's all about you."

Neptune took a moment to let all the information sink in. His immediate assumption that Ryman was here for Carly in a romantic way was derailed by the man's frank admission. That meant he was truly just here to support his work partner, although if the few things Carly'd let drop were to be believed, things the man had reinforced just now with his words, they probably had a much tighter relationship than normal coworkers. It was gratifying to know he hadn't misread her excitement at the idea of riding behind him on the bike, and her making a point to call the one person in her life who'd understand was not lost on Neptune.

He took a deep breath to give himself a moment to mentally adjust, then strode back to where Ryman stood next to the bike. Hand outstretched, he gripped the man's wrist in a warrior's greeting. "Lemme start over, man. Sorry. We'd be honored to have you ride with us." He clenched his left fist, thudding it against his chest over his nameplate. "Call me Neptune, not Dobbs. Breathe easy, brother."

"Neptune," Ryman returned, grip tightening. "I've got a road name, too, if you wanna use it."

"Hit me with it, and I'll let you know." Neptune made to release the man, stymied when Ryman's hand didn't relax. "All ears here."

"Monday."

Neptune blinked and felt his head tilt to the side. "Come again?" He leaned a little closer. "I didn't catch that." An engine revved nearby, exhaust sounds ringing off nearby buildings. Ryman's mouth moved, but the words were drowned out by the noise. "Still didn't hear you, man."

Mouth spreading wide in a grin, Ryman shook his head and repeated himself. "Monday, man. Monday."

"Monday? Like an *Addams Family* reference? Like Wednesday?" He shook his head. "But Monday?"

"No, man. Just Monday." Ryman shrugged and dropped his hold, leaving Neptune's hand hanging in the air for a moment.

"Monday." Neptune laughed softly. "Goes against the grain to ask, man, but I gotta know where that one came from."

"Everybody hates Monday." The man's mouth pulled sideways, trying to hide a return of his grin. "I'm kind of an asshole."

"Oh, Jesus." Neptune laughed loud, head back, without trying to contain his humor. A moment later, he was given the unexpected reward of a small hand touching his waist, heat pressing up against his side. He looked down to see Carly standing next to him, her eyes on his face as she smiled up at him. "Hey, there." He gestured towards Ryman—fuck if he'd be able to call him Monday in his head—who was walking around the back of his bike with arms out. "Your favorite asshole's here."

"Ryman." Her voice was low and soft, carrying notes of surprised pleasure. "I didn't expect to see you today." She leaned into the man's embrace, and Neptune heard her whisper, "It's a little overwhelming. So many people came, just for him."

"And you, Carly. Take what's being offered, sister. Take it and run with it, because having this kind of family can be a powerful thing." Ryman's gaze met Neptune's over her head. "There's some good men here, ready to stand beside you if you let them." A buzz set up in Neptune's head, growing until it overwhelmed the noises around them. He stared as Carly shifted, her head turning just enough to look at him, eyes staying on his face as she nodded, her hair shifting and moving against Ryman's chest. "Now." Ryman straightened and turned her, arm around her shoulders. "Where do I sign up for this shindig?"

Neptune watched them walk away, uncertain what this warmth in his chest meant until he saw Carly's head twist around, fingers lifting in a fluttering wave as she mouthed, "Back in a minute."

Fuck.

He couldn't get hung up on Gibby's girl. It shouldn't matter how funny or fierce she was, how deeply she'd loved her father or the depth of trust she'd granted Neptune multiple times now by exposing her pain and fear. He couldn't get hung up on any woman. He knew his brothers depended on him to have full focus on their joint goal of finding Gibby's murderers and taking their own brand of justice.

Moving slowly, he deliberately turned his back on the registration area where Ryman had led Carly and swept the crowd with a glance. Monk stood near the shed Blade used for his mechanic jobs for the club, and Neptune wasted no time making his way that direction.

"Brother," he muttered, arm thrust out for a handshake. "Half an hour until kickstands up. We ready to go?"

Monk stood tall and nodded, his gaze traveling from Neptune's face over his shoulder, probably landing directly on where Carly stood with Ryman. His brother gave him the out needed and ignored that aspect of what would be happening today, focusing instead on his job and role: road captain.

"Yeah, we're good. Staging's been happening steadily as folks register, and our boys aren't letting them into line without a wristband. No anonymous tagalongs today."

Monk tipped his head towards the shed, and Neptune realized the steady stream of profanities he'd been hearing were coming from that direction. "Blade's rigging up some Bluetooth shit for half a dozen of us including you and me, so we can communicate with the hoppers and sweeps."

He nodded. "Still no word from Putnam?" The statie had promised to do what he could to gain approval to authorize an escort for the ride, but they hadn't heard anything from him yet. Monk shook his head. "Then we assume we're unescorted and have to block traffic ourselves. Good job on the ears, man."

"We're better off on our own, anyway." Monk's features darkened, anger sweeping over his face. "Motherfuckers should be better spending their time finding the assholes who did this."

"Honestly?" Neptune paused, waiting for Monk's nod. "I'm hoping they don't find them first."

A hand gripped his shoulder, followed by the thudding of a closed fist against his back. He turned to see Wolf had walked up beside him, the same anger shadowing his expression. "Right there with you, brother. Freaks take care of Freaks' shit, and we both know it."

There was a rumble of a bike nearby, and Neptune turned to see Ryman idling his way to the end of a row of bikes. He made a split-second decision and shoved two fingers in his mouth, whistling shrilly. Every prospect within earshot looked up, gazes homing in on him. He pointed to the biker and then to a spot farther up the line, directly behind the Borderline Freaks' spot at the head of the column. A thumbs-up from one of the prospects preceded the instructions being passed to Ryman, who glanced at Neptune before acknowledging the change in assignment and shifting trajectory.

"He's a friend of Carly's" was all he offered to the two men looking at him curiously.

"I can't get the fucking things to work right." Blade stuck his head out of the shed's doorway as he yelled at them. "Static and ignorance, I'm awash in both." He tapped the side of his head, and Neptune realized he had an earpiece in. "Nothing. Not a damn thing. Fakes and liars. Assholes."

"Let me try." The feminine voice was one that had already etched its way into his psyche, and Neptune didn't have to turn and look to know it was Carly. She approached Blade with one hand out. "I've worked with all kinds of equipment. They can be really fussy."

"Tell me about it, little sister." Blade's mutter was quiet as he passed Carly several of the earpieces he had in his hand. "I've got a bench inside if you need somewhere to work on them."

"Yeah." She sounded distracted, already dialed in on the devices. She walked past where Neptune stood with the other men and gave him a little chin lift, bottom lip trapped between her teeth as she turned the earpieces over and over in her hand. "That'd be good."

Blade and Carly disappeared into the shed, the murmur of their conversation drifting out occasionally. Neptune startled when a hand landed on his arm, Monk's fingers tightening and loosening. He hadn't realized he'd blocked out everything, trying to make out what was being said. It wasn't even jealousy, because Blade was totally devoted to his woman. It was the look on Carly's face that said she'd just entered a place that made her entirely happy. *Something to figure out.*

Ryman's voice broke his train of thought, and Neptune twisted to see the big man walking up beside him. He greeted him with a nod, then quickly made introductions, shaking his head as he muttered the man's self-proclaimed road name.

Predictably, Monk was the one who latched on to the moniker, asking in a voice an octave higher than normal, "Monday? No shit, man? From Picklewood?" Something in his tone captured Neptune's attention, and he watched Ryman's features smooth over as if with a paintbrush, all animation leaving the man's face within a breath. "Heard good things about you, man. Welcome and well met."

Something else to figure out.

Blade's laughter was brash and loud coming from the shed, as were his hoots of celebration. He stuck his head out, then ducked away again for a moment, allowing Carly to precede him from the building. They were laughing and talking companionably, and Neptune was reminded of the hours spent at Gibby's place. *Her place, now.* It didn't matter that Gibby'd left it to the club. If Carly wanted it, she deserved to have whatever of her father she could hold on to.

"Carly girl's got the touch. There's a controller needed to link them all together, and I didn't know what the damn thing was. I'll have it in my pocket during the ride and we should be golden. She says it's got a few-mile radius, so easy breezy." He wrapped an arm around her shoulder, tugging her sideways against him. "Good job, little sister."

Color crept into her cheeks, and Carly darted a smile at Blade, deftly separating herself from his hold without seeming to do so. Neptune noticed because he was watching closely, and he knew Ryman had seen when the man cut a glance at him. They shared a quick grimace. Then Monk lifted his voice in a shout.

"Ten minutes until the blessing. Get to your bikes. We'll start 'em up right after, and roll." He clasped the forearm of each man in their little group, including Ryman. "Shiny side up."

Each man murmured his version of the benediction, the BFMC members accepting an earpiece from Blade before they walked to their bikes. A moment passed, and Neptune was left with Carly and Ryman, looking back and forth between them as they seemed to have a silent conversation filled with lip quirks and brow lifts.

"If you're finished..." He cleared his throat and was unsurprised when both Carly and Ryman turned those completely blank and placid expressions in his direction. "I need to get ready. Carly, I've got a helmet for you, regardless which bike you choose to ride on." He gestured to where his ride was parked. "It's just over there."

"I told you—"

"Is this you uninviting me?" Carly's soft question cut off Ryman's argument.

"No. But Ryman's your partner." He tried not to put any special emphasis on the word, keeping what Ryman had told him in mind. "And you might be more comfortable with a known component." He shrugged and took a step backwards, lifting the earpiece up and fitting it into place. "Up to you. Lady's choice."

"I'll ride with you, if it's all the same." Her voice was firm, brooking no argument, and he didn't give any.

A warmth crept over him, and he fought with himself to take her words at face value. He stretched his hand out, gratified when she quickly met his palm with hers, fingers threading together.

"Sounds good."

Six

Carly

It had been a while since she'd ridden on the back of a bike, but Carly found it surprisingly easy to slip back into the rhythm. The most challenging part of everything was the enforced physical closeness between her body and Neptune's, something she'd initially tried to minimize by sitting back slightly while gripping either side of his waist. He'd put a stop to that early on, leaning back and telling her to "Slide up, honey. Get friendly. We're gonna be on here for a while." Then he'd put actions to his words, gripping behind each of her knees and sliding her as close to him as he could.

They'd taken off right after that, without her having a chance to adjust, which she suspected was his intent.

The farther they got into the ride, the easier it became, until she wasn't thinking about how awkward it should have been and was just appreciating the beauty of the scenery flashing past. They rode through woods thick enough that the temperature dropped several degrees in the shade of the overhanging trees, bursting back out into dazzling sunlight and a heat more than enough to shake the chill off her skin. A pair of horses must've heard the bikes coming, running up to the fence that separated their field and the bordering road before turning and racing along, kicking up their heels as the bikes outstripped the horses' eager strides.

Minutes passed and she slowly relaxed, leaning against Neptune, swaying with him as he maneuvered the bike around curve after curve. They slowed and she sat up, looking over his shoulder to see an intersection coming up. Two motorcycles blasted past them in the other lane, swooping to either side of the crossing, effectively blocking traffic from interfering with the double columns of bikes. It had been the same at the other intersections, three teams of riders she'd come to recognize. She twisted and looked behind them, seeing Monk and Amanda riding just to the right of Neptune's bike, with Wolf and Rose and Blade and Jenn making up the couples on the next set of bikes.

Craning her neck, she caught a glimpse of Ryman several rows back. It seemed like he was laughing as he shouted something to the rider next to him, but when he saw her looking, his expression sobered and he lifted a hand in a brief wave she returned.

Neptune's hand on her lower leg made her turn around again and lean closer. He'd done that several times today, each when he'd wanted to tell her something. This was no different.

Over the buffeting wind, she heard him demand, "Get my phone out. It's in my vest pocket."

Hands on his waist, she considered the request. Trust was involved. She'd have to let go of him with her hands, leaving her more vulnerable to the bike's movement. She pulled herself tight against his back, then clamped her thighs around his hips, holding firmly. Her hands snaked around his chest on either side, and she worked by feel to find the rectangle that would identify the phone's position. It was in an inside pocket, and she carefully unsnapped one set of closures before reaching inside. Her palm spread across his chest, and the hardness under her fingertips reminded her of those moments when she'd given way to her grief, cradled against him. Carly shook it off and retrieved the phone, fumbling to close the snap until she felt it pop into place.

"Okay," she yelled over his shoulder. "Got it."

"Get a video of the column. I wanna have something of today to keep."

Her stomach pitched and sank, and her fingers shook until she was afraid she'd drop the phone. He wanted something to remember her father's memorial ride. Like the home movies and videos he'd shared with her the other evening, it would be something more than a fading memory of the wind and trusted men at his back, the honor of the many guests who'd showed for the ride. He wanted tangible proof of the overwhelming support and love the biker community had for Gibby, and by extension, the Borderline Freaks MC as a whole.

She fought the emotions for a moment, resting her helmet against his back, then took a deep breath and opened her eyes. Familiarizing herself with the controls, she clamped her thighs around his hips again and leaned backwards slightly; then, with her arms over Neptune's shoulders, she held the camera in front, aimed it at him in selfie mode and hit the red button. After capturing several seconds of that closeup, the image including her face framed by the helmet hovering over his shoulder, she lifted her arms and tipped her head to watch the screen as riders behind them came into view. Several of the men lifted a hand in solemn acknowledgment, and many of the women riding with them waved. Carly angled the phone to see farther back up the column, and farther still, realizing it extended well beyond what she could see.

He touched her leg and she jerked, fitting herself against his back, camera out in front again. "Gonna pull off, want you to keep filming. Get the whole ride as it passes, okay?" She nodded and knew he'd seen it on the screen when he grinned at her. Lifting a hand, he touched the earpiece he wore and told the other leaders what he was planning to do. At the next intersection, they became the bike swooping off on the right-hand side to block traffic, and she quickly flipped the camera to forward mode, scanning the riders as they swept past in a roar of exhaust and excited shouts.

Minutes ticked by, and they continued to sit in the road as hundreds of motorcycles made their way through. Carly glanced across the intersection and somehow wasn't surprised to see Ryman was the one blocking traffic on the other side. When the final bike rolled past, she draped her arms across Neptune's shoulders, framed the two of them on the screen, and angled the camera so it captured Ryman in the background. "Thank you," she mouthed, then turned her head and impulsively brushed her lips across Neptune's cheek.

She ended the recording and tucked the phone deep into the pocket of her jeans. When she wrapped her arms around his waist, he draped his left elbow over her knee and cupped his hand around her calf possessively. This wasn't a move to get her attention as it had been earlier in the day. This was a comfortable connection between two people.

Carly wasn't sure how she felt about that.

Seven

Neptune

He swept his gaze across the faces gathered in the field behind the clubhouse, marking the members who remained. It was most of them, which was surprising since it had been a long, full day. The clock crept up on midnight, and the fire was finally beginning to burn down, Monk having put a moratorium on adding to the blaze about an hour ago. He'd stayed but had sent Amanda home earlier, shaking his head when Neptune had asked after her.

At the picnic table nearest the clubhouse, Neptune spied Carly. She was seated facing his direction, and this time, as he'd found every time he looked at her over the past hour, the woman's gaze had been parked directly on where he stood. Ryman was next to her, a buffer against the off-side approach by anyone. That was a considerate move, given how stressed out Carly seemed.

He would have expected the honor paid to her father today to have eased her somewhat. It was hard to lose anyone, much less a parent, but knowing how revered and well-liked Gibby had been should have lightened her load. Instead, it had seemed to double, maybe triple, the weight of her grief.

When they'd pulled back into the clubhouse parking lot, she'd remained in place at his back for a moment, her arms tight around his waist. As he'd parked and killed the bike's engine, she'd stripped off the helmet and run her fingers through her hair. Then she'd placed her hands on his shoulders and pulled, drawing him back against her. A gust of heated air across his ear told him how close her mouth was when she thanked him; then those supple lips eased forwards, and she pressed another kiss to his cheek. The second such offering from her today.

He hadn't been prepared for her exit off the bike, having been frozen in place enjoying the heat of her body against his. But Ryman had been right there, hand out, supporting her as she stepped down off the passenger pegs. Neptune had watched the big man tuck her hand into the bend of his elbow, then escort her between the clusters of men and women stretching after a long ride. They'd rounded the end of the clubhouse and disappeared from view.

It had taken time for Neptune to work his way around to the back, as protocol demanded he personally regreet and thank every club that had members present. Sorting out the ranking officers, determining the level of gratitude to express, extending an offer to remain for the back-lot party, and then closing out with handshakes all around—doing that times nearly three dozen clubs, he hadn't been surprised when the food was already being consumed by the time he made it out back of the clubhouse.

Prospects and members had already been sternly warned about behavior and expectations, and he was glad to see that even now, at this late hour, they'd held their shit. Not a one of his men was drunk to the point they'd be a weakness. There were a few tents pitched along one edge of the field, which told him not every attendee had held the same level of control. Still, that too was what he'd primed the prospects to do, helping ensure there'd be no issues with drunk driving traffic stops. The last thing the club needed right now was some kind of a bullshit charge about the clubhouse serving as an unlicensed bar.

"Officer church tomorrow, right?" Monk's question came from left field, and Neptune squinted at him for a moment before nodding slowly. "Afternoon or evening?"

"Tempted to put an 18:00 time on it. What do you think?" Neptune watched Wolf walk up behind Monk, saw them share a glance. "What the fuck's going on?"

"Told you he'd catch wind." Wolf shook his head. "Might as well just spill it, man."

Monk's head turned back and forth, his gaze scanning the crowd much as Neptune's had. "Nothing's even for sure yet."

"What's not for sure?" Blade stepped around Neptune, planting himself in the only empty part of their circle. "It's for sure late, and my woman's already fussin' about goin' home."

"I sent Amanda home already." Monk's shoulders shifted, and he swayed in place. "Makes me nervous having her there alone, though."

"Same." Wolf lifted his chin, pointing to the table where Carly sat with the other women. "I'm of a mind I want to keep my eyes on her. We just don't know what they'd be willing to do."

"They've come after the women before." Blade shrugged. "I told Jenn she had to suck it up and deal with it, because her moving back and forth alone ain't happening."

"Only reason I felt okay with Amanda heading out was because a couple of ladies from her grief support group are staying over." Monk shifted again, unease clear on his face. "She's..." His voice trailed off for a moment before coming back, stronger. "She's pregnant. I didn't want her alone."

Neptune's shoulders went back, and he stared at Monk. His brother and Amanda hadn't followed the smoothest trail to where they were. It had taken the two wounded souls a long time to decide they were worth love again.

Neptune had stood at their side when they'd gotten married, the civil service at the courthouse taking forever as the fussy little official had tacked on several paragraphs of narration to the usual service. As far as he knew, neither Monk nor Amanda had talked about kids, so this was a shock. "Congratulations, brother. Precious addition to your family. That's good news, man. Really good news." He reached out and clapped a hand on Monk's shoulder, gripping tightly. "Y'all excited about this?"

Monk nodded, lips curving as he grinned through his beard. "Yeah, it's a good thing. We hadn't been trying for long. The good stuff just happened nice and fast." He reached up and clasped Neptune's arm. "She told Gibby her suspicion the weekend before...before everything went sideways. He was really pleased."

"I bet he was, Monk. Awesome news. Congrats, brother." Wolf stepped close and pulled Monk into a clinch. "Me and Rose better get a move on it, so mine and your kids can grow up together. I told her last night we've waited long enough. First it was her training, then her probationary period, then her first year. It's time."

"It is time," Monk agreed. He cut a glance at Blade. "How about you and Jenn?"

"If Jenn wants kids, I'll make it happen. Not a serious topic at our house yet." Blade slugged Monk's arm, hitting him hard enough to pull a wince from the bigger man. "Figures you'd be the one to blaze ahead."

"Yeah." Monk's smile was edged with a darker emotion. "But after what happened to Gibby, we've got to get our asses in gear and sort a terminal solution. I'm ready to do whatever the club needs. I'm a Freak through and through, and I'll stand by my brothers without question."

"Well said, but let's keep this for tomorrow's church." Neptune glanced at the picnic table, surprised to see Ryman seated there alone. He looked around the yard, not seeing Carly. "You guys see where Carly went?"

"She was just right there with Rose." Blade turned and cursed. "Where the hell'd my woman go? Where's Jenn?"

Ryman saw them staring and glanced around. Neptune noted the moment when he realized the women were all gone. He was up from the table in a flash, head on a swivel as he glared into the corners of the yard. Neptune was on him in seconds, hand plastered against Ryman's chest as he let his momentum carry them backwards until Ryman's back crashed against the clubhouse wall. Fist in the man's shirt, he asked, "What'd she say? Just before you let her walk away, what'd she say?"

"She got a text. All of them did. Nothing pinged wrong, man. She got a text and looked up laughing, and asked if Jenn and Rose were walking inside, too." Ryman shook his head, and Neptune saw his pupils dilate, covering his eyes in darkness. "I figured it was some of that shit where women hit the head in herds." He fumbled at his pocket, and Neptune released him, taking a long step back to put distance between them. Not that he expected Ryman to retaliate, but he'd make it harder for him to do so at least. "Seven minutes. Seven and a half."

Neptune sent Monk into the clubhouse with a tip of his head, and Blade to the front parking lot and the mechanic shed with a pair of members at his back. Ryman had pulled out his phone and was tapping furiously at it, navigating from screen to screen as if looking for something. Neptune got the attention of a few other members and had them combing through the crowd and tents, quietly but thoroughly. He did all this with a sinking feeling in his gut that every search would turn up empty. *Fruitless*, he thought. Whatever coordinated effort had swept the women away wouldn't be recovered by the same tactics used to locate a lost toddler's shoe.

"Goddammit." Ryman's low muttering peaked, his frustration coming through. "I got nothing. Literally nothing. There are only like three fucking CCTV feeds in the whole town, and they've all been smeared with petroleum jelly." He stared at Neptune. "Do you have anything?"

"Yeah." Wolf was intent on his phone. "I got something."

Neptune opened his mouth to respond when something in the pocket of his vest buzzed. He dug out the earpiece and held it between his fingers and thumb. It vibrated again, sounds coming from it, and Neptune shoved it into his ear. He wasn't prepared for what he heard.

LACK OF IN-BETWEEN

Eight

Carly

Carly'd known what she'd be walking into when she had chosen to accept the instructions at face value. The initial text she'd received said to make sure her companions accompanied her, and after having learned about Rose's military background and current posting during their earlier conversation, it hadn't been a hard decision. The second text had come in at the same time the other women looked at their phones, and Carly had put a stamp on how things would go when she'd drawn the women's attention to her with an over-the-top response that wouldn't give Ryman anything to worry about.

Now, however, she was rethinking the instinct that always drove her to manage her own cases.

The inside of the cargo van was not completely dark, fortunately. There was a solid panel between where they sat on the floor and the driver's cabin, and the single window in the back door was covered by a grate. The glass in the window was painted a dark gray, scrapes through the covering only allowing the tiniest bit of illumination around the edges of the seal. Tiny, but enough.

"Where do you think they're taking us?" Jenn sounded angry, the tone in her voice hard-edged and clipped.

Good, Carly thought. *Hold on to that little bit of pissed off.* She answered the question though, because the three of them needed to be in sync while keeping their captors in the dark as much as possible. "Probably to my dad's house." She shook her head in wide sweeps, making sure both Jenn and Rose saw her. "Woods," she mouthed, hoping they'd understand.

That initial text had held more information than her captors probably knew.

They got off too easy. That had meant Neptune, Wolf, Blade, and Monk, she was certain. She knew the tipoff about her father's death had only been sent to them, but they'd wisely involved the entire club. The men descending upon the woods in a huge group had probably derailed the killers' plans.

You're going to fix this for us or go like your old man. The killers thought she had some sway over the club's leadership, probably because of who her father had been.

They hadn't been watching closely, or they'd have made it a more personal threat about Neptune. She'd not been able to keep her eyes off him after the ride, watching him easily accept the grief the men handed him, giving them back comfort and ease even while seeking her out with his gaze again and again. It hadn't just been her impacted by their time on the motorcycle today—or by the sense of rightness with every moment spent in his presence.

Bring their women or it'll be worse for you. That sentence was the most damning one, because it meant the abductors had been fed information from someone at the party. How else would they have known she'd even met Jenn and Rose, much less been seated with them at the exact moment the text came in? Scanning the groups of men and women standing around the clubhouse's backyard, her gaze had landed on a man. One amongst dozens, he'd held a beer bottle just like so many others, but he'd also had a phone in his hand—and his eyes on the table where she sat. Carly took a discreet picture of him with her phone as she'd laughed and urged Jenn and Rose to their feet, only then noticing Ryman's attention was on the same man.

Don't fuck up or it'll go bad for her. That had been the final sentence of that first text, and it had confused her for a moment. That confusion was cleared up with the second text. A picture of a woman, bruises not hidden by her tear-smeared makeup, with a man's hand cruelly gripping her jaw to angle her face to the camera. It had been accompanied by a single sentence. ***Van's out front***.

"Who's the woman in the picture?" Carly murmured the question quietly, hoping the two women would understand why.

When Rose answered her back the same way, only breathing out the answer, she knew Rose at least had gotten the idea. "Darla. She's friends with the club." Friends didn't mean the woman was involved with a particular member, but Carly didn't let herself dig too deep into what it meant until Rose continued. "Neptune's a favorite of hers."

Oh, hell no. Schooling herself to stillness, she looked at Rose in time to see a pained expression cross her features. Not able to stifle the need to stake her claim, she whispered back, "I'm thinkin', after the past couple of days, that's no longer the case." The smile Rose flashed her vindicated Carly's emotion even as she stuffed it deep inside a box far back in her psyche. She—they all had to focus. "I've got one gun on me."

Jenn scrambled closer and put her mouth next to Carly's ear as she whispered, "Mace in my bag."

Rose was right there, nodding to indicate she'd heard Jenn, too. Then Rose helped keep things into perspective by reminding Carly, "Remember? I'm a cop. Shacked up with a BFMC officer. In case you're wondering, Wolf'll be all over this." Her next words were a surprise, however, "There's a tracker on my phone, a Taser in my bag, and I've got my Sig on my six."

Carly pulled back and stared at Rose, who grinned back at her. She leaned in and asked, "Bad guys know you're a cop?" Rose shook her head, then shrugged, which wasn't the answer Carly would have wanted, but was a maybe she'd take. "Ryman—" At the blank stares from the two women, she remembered how he'd introduced himself to them. "Monday's my partner. I work…" It took a moment to find the right words. "Security in the private sector, and he's my backup. He'll be all over it, too."

"Well, shit." Rose wrinkled her nose and kept up the theme of bravado that Carly prayed would help carry them through whatever was coming. "I hope we get to deal with the baddies before our men get here."

The van slowed and turned, the surface underneath the wheels changing to something uneven that had gravel and small rocks pinging against the undercarriage. Carly braced herself, head tilted to the side to try to hear anything that might signal what would be waiting for them at the end of this drive. Scraping sounds against the sides of the van validated her initial instincts, and she saw Rose give her a tiny nod, indicating she'd made the same connection.

They were in the woods where her father had died, undoubtedly abducted by the hands of the men who'd killed him. There were a variety of things these men did not know, including her well-honed skill set and those of her companions.

It couldn't have been a more perfect setup if Carly had done it herself.

***

Neptune

Ryman and Wolf spoke nearly at the same time, their words overlapping over the earpiece.

"Carly's stopped moving."

"Rose's phone is in Waltham's Woods."

A shiver made its way up Neptune's spine, making his breaths come short.

Waltham's Woods was where Gibby had died.

The party had come to a screeching halt when it became clear the three women weren't at the clubhouse anymore. Ryman had quickly volunteered that he had tracking on Carly, not disclosing how exactly, and Wolf wasted no time in verifying the device he'd put into Rose's phone was still working. Carly had moved out of range for the earpiece to keep transmitting, but the conversation he'd heard from the women had been chilling. There'd been a brief strategic meeting, and at the end, Neptune dispatched fully a third of the men to follow Monk home, instructed to stay there and protect Amanda.

The rest of the men were with him, in a convoy of motorcycles followed by a couple of trucks. He didn't want to think about the need for those vehicles, at least not until he had Carly safe again. There was no room for emotion in him right now, just the mission and ensuring a successful outcome. *We'll get them back. I know we will.*

Reaching up, he tapped the earpiece and spoke. "Not leading my men to slaughter." He remembered the silence of those woods, the trees trapping all sound and muffling it so he hadn't been able to hear the cops rolling up the lane but had seen their lights instead. "Bikes are gonna be too fuckin' loud. We'll stop at the farm just before and stage out of there. Take a walk through the woods." That would put him and his men with the best advantage. "And we're not leaving until those women are safe and the assholes are put in their place."

"What's their place, brother?" Wolf's voice was strong, vibrating through the words, feeding Neptune a line he needed so he could state it plain.

"Ain't among the living, I tell you what. Earning themselves a short shift in a six by two, and we'll dig that mother as deep as we need to." He threw up a fist, pumping it twice. "Gonna get it for Gibby, man. Get what the man deserves, and we need. *Vengeance.*"

In his mirror, he saw a sea of raised fists over the lines of rumbling bikes and lifted his chin, rocking his throttle a little farther over, picking up speed for the final miles to their turnoff.

***

Carly

The van had been parked for only a few minutes—Carly would estimate less than five—but the silence around them was profound. Other than the rocking of the suspension as the driver had exited the vehicle, she hadn't heard anything.

They're playing with us.

"Fuck this," she muttered, lunging towards the door and yanking on the handle. To her surprise, it moved smoothly, the unexpected click of the latch disengaging shockingly loud. Oh yeah, they were playing. The problem was, they didn't really know who they had on the other end of the stick. Carly looked over her shoulder at the two women, both on their feet now, crouched behind her. Jenn had the Taser in one hand. It was a stab and shock model, and Carly marked her thumb resting beside the button that would light up the two prongs with an immobilizing dose of electricity. Rose's gun was in her hand, safety off, finger laid alongside the trigger. Carly adjusted her grip on the small pistol she held, reminding herself how few shots she had. "Let's roll, ladies."

Darkness lay in front of them as she swung the door open wide to a seemingly endless expanse of woods. The van's headlights had been left on, so behind them was a shining glow. Carly ducked low, angling her head around the vehicle as she saw Rose do the same on the opposite side. Spotlighted in the steady beams was a woman standing on a chair, rope reaching from her neck to a thick tree limb overhead. She had her hands in front of her face, working at the ropes binding her wrists with her teeth, but Carly had no doubts that this was the woman from the image: Darla.

"Shit." The rough whisper meant Rose must have seen her too. Carly looked back to see Rose was still in place, but the woman was nearly vibrating in her need to get to Darla. Carly understood the urge but knew it had to be a trap. She gripped Rose's arm, got her attention, and then motioned down. They stared at each other for a moment, then fell to their stomachs at nearly the same time. Carly shifted to the side to see around the van's tires and felt a thrill as she saw two sets of boots directly in front of the van. If they'd rushed to help the woman, the men would have been at their backs with the blinding lights of the van to up their advantage.

Yanking on Jenn's arm got her on the ground between Carly and Rose, and the moment she saw the men, she understood, immediately moving to crawl through the dirt underneath the vehicle. Carly put her hand on Jenn's shoulder and got her attention before leaning close to whisper, "Aim high, over the top of their boots. It'll work okay through the jeans but not leather." Jenn nodded and faced forwards again, using elbows and toes to work her way towards the men.

Rose stared at her, then jerked her head towards the front of the van. "Slow and steady," she whispered, echoing what Carly had been thinking. "Between us, we've got this."

Carly gripped the back of Rose's neck, pulling her close so their foreheads touched. "I knew I liked you." Rose grinned at her words; then the expression faded, leaving a look of pure determination behind.

"Let's go save the day."

***

Neptune

Ryman wasn't fucking around, trotting through the woods, deftly dodging branches and deadfalls, and in the process leading Neptune on a straight path forwards. He'd latched onto Ryman's vest, twisting his fingers tight and keeping hold of the denim as the line of men spread out behind and beside them. Wolf was off to the right, headed the same direction, which was proof enough for Neptune that Ryman had a lock on Carly's position just like he said he did.

Neptune saw the glow ahead as Ryman slowed. As he released his grip on the man, Neptune used the light to study the ground in front of him and pick his path. They were both moving soundlessly, revealing they'd had similar training. As the light slowly resolved into the headlights of a vehicle, he realized it was parked in the same clearing where Gibby had been found. A dark shape moved alongside the van, the form making its way towards where two men stood staring at the tree that was between where he stood and them. He moved to the side slightly and saw a figure hanging from the tree. *Jesus.* It took a moment to realize it was a woman—and she wasn't hanging, but standing on a stool of some kind. There was a noose around her neck, though, and the slightest stumble would turn things bad in an instant.

Several things happened in rapid sequence. One of the men screamed, his voice shrill and pained as he arched backwards before falling to the side. The other man turned to look at his companion just as the figure rounded the front of the van directly behind him, an arm rising and falling with force. Whatever had been used to hit the man with was enough to knock him to his knees but not incapacitate him entirely. The figure moved into the light, and he realized it was Carly just as her hand lifted, aiming a small pistol directly at the man's chest. *Jesus.*

A figure came around the other side of the van and rolled the prone body over, dropping a knee in the middle of his back. *Rose.*

Another woman shimmied out from under the van, and he saw Jenn's expression of horror as she raised her arm to point at the woman who'd been standing on the stool. It had tipped to one side during the fracas, and she was on tiptoes trying to keep herself from choking.

Neptune and Ryman reached the woman at the same time, and in a surreal re-creation of cutting Gibby down, they circled her legs and hips with their arms, lifting and holding her in place. Wolf pushed past them to get to the women while Blade paused to set the stool upright, climbing quickly before he stretched with a knife in hand and sawed through the rope with effort. Only a moment later, the woman was free, and Neptune released his hold, giving her to Ryman, who eased her to the ground. Neptune looked around and found Carly, still holding her gun on the man while Wolf zip-tied his arms behind his back. The other man was showing signs of life, but too late, as Rose was finishing securing his ankles to his wrists.

"Get used to this." Ryman's words didn't make sense, and he twisted to look at the man, locking gazes for a moment. "She doesn't need rescuing often. My main job is usually just cleaning up after her."

"Neptune." At the hoarse shout, he turned to see Carly walking towards him, her labored breathing belying the gun held casually at her side. "Come tell me if it's them. Please tell me it's them."

He got close, cupped her jaw in one hand, and steadied her, wrapping his fingers around the back of her skull. "You're fuckin' amazing." Leaning in, he brushed his lips across hers once, twice—and on the third pass, she was the one kissing him, pursuing his mouth with a darting lap of her tongue. "You're okay?"

"Yeah." Her breathing was still uneven, but he hoped it was for a different reason. "Your entrance was extremely well-timed."

"I aim to please." Her mouth curved in a smile at his words, but it faded quickly.

"Tell me if it's them. This is the place where it happened, right? They brought us right back here? What stupid fucking idiots." He pulled back slightly at the vehemence of her words, giving her space. Carly's lips thinned and her chin bumped unsteadily for a moment, tears welling in her eyes. "They killed my daddy right here, didn't they?"

"Yeah, baby." Neptune slipped his hands up and down her arms slowly, keeping his gaze focused on her eyes. He hated seeing her struggle with her emotions, longed to pull her close as he had in the clubhouse earlier today, giving her a safe place to let go. *I can do that later*, he thought. Now was not the right time for anything other than brutal honesty. "What do you need from me? I'll give you whatever you need, Carly. You want to deal with them, we'll make it happen. I fuckin' swear to you. You want them gone, they're ghosts."

She stared at him for so long he thought he'd lost her. Whether to memories or plans, he didn't care, as long as she came back to him. Bending closer, he regained the distance he'd given to her, and with mouths nearly touching, he breathed her in, watching. Finally, he asked cautiously, "Carly?"

She blinked, and her pupils dilated, then narrowed to pinpoints as she focused on his face. Her voice was steady and strong as she clipped, "I want justice."

Neptune nodded, the movement ghosting his lips across hers. He made a promise to her in that moment. "Anything you need, you got it." Arms folded around her shoulders, he pulled her against him as he stood straight, staring out at the men—Gibby's men, his men—once again clustered in black-leather clad groups around the clearing. This time the body they'd cut from the tree was still breathing, not cold and still. *That's a win right there.* Ryman stood near Darla, who'd been moved out from under the tree. Neptune saw the stool lying on its side, left behind in the dirt. Rose and Jenn were next to the van, bracketed on either side by their men.

"Wolf," he called, pitching his voice so every person in the clearing could hear him. Carly shifted closer, and her arms encircled his waist, holding as tight to him as he was her. "Get Rose to call it in, yeah?" To Carly, he said, "We'll have to stay until they take statements. Could be a couple of hours. When we're done here, I want you to come to my place. Let me take care of you."

"You don't have to—"

"I know." He cut her off, but not unkindly. "I know I don't have to. What you need to understand is that I want to, Carly. Scared the fuck outta me when I realized you were gone."

"I bet the other guys were scared, too."

"Hell yeah. Nothing but terror for any of us. I can't imagine a man I know not losing his shit when someone he cares for is in danger." His immediate response seemed to surprise her, and he stared down into her face as she looked up at him. "If Ryman hadn't had that tracking gizmo, I'd have lost my mind."

"About Jenn and Rose?"

The uncertainty in her gaze tore something loose in his chest, and he groaned softly as he gathered her against his chest, molding her to his body.

"No, sweetheart. Well, yeah, I worried about them too. But you were the one I couldn't quit thinking about. The things you told me the other night, stuff you survived, all the good you've done in the world, I couldn't imagine anything happening to you." He rested his cheek against the crown of her head, struggling to control his breathing. "I mean, I could imagine it all, that was the worst part. Not knowing. Scared the hell out of me."

"So you, what? Came to rescue me?" That fine tremor was back in her voice, and he hated hearing it. "Me?"

"Ryman told me you don't require saving often." His words startled a laugh out of her, and he smiled to hear it. "Don't mean I won't try it, if I feel there's a need." Eyes closed, he trusted the nearby men to keep them safe as he focused on Carly. Within the safety of the darkness behind his lids, he put his mouth next to her ear and laid it out for her. "I found something in you that matches me, Carly. I've never felt like this before, wanna see how this plays out. But honestly? Just between you me and the fence post over there," another laugh rattled through her, this one less forced, "I don't expect it to play out anytime soon. I've looked and looked and never found a match. Not even close. Kinda figured there just wasn't a person out there for me. Then you stalk into your daddy's kitchen and sweep the legs out from under that thinking. You might not need saving, but honey, I do." He took a slow breath, swallowed hard, and said a quick prayer before he asked her a question that meant everything to him. "You gonna save me, Carly?"

She stirred in his arms, and he raised up in time to meet her mouth with his, opening for her as she lapped at his lips, chasing her tongue back into her mouth to tangle and stroke along it there. Long minutes passed as he kissed her, the caress renewing over and again as she angled her chin and tilted her neck, giving him a target to chase. He slanted his mouth across hers a final time, lifting to look down at her, surprised at the slashes of red and white light that danced across her face. The staties had shown while they'd been otherwise occupied, and neither Neptune nor Carly had noticed.

She lifted a hand and stroked across his cheek, her thumb toying with his lips as she smiled and watched herself touch him. He pressed a kiss to the pad of a finger, then dared a quick nip, kissing her again when she laughed.

"Guessin' that's a yes?"

She nodded, gaze locked with his.

"Good."

***

Carly

It was much longer than the couple of hours Neptune had predicted before they were finally released by the police. Putnam hadn't been unkind as he'd questioned her; in fact, it had been one of the easiest debriefings she'd ever dealt with. Carly knew Ryman felt the same way when she caught him watching her from across the clearing, a broad grin on his face. The woman, Darla, had been cuddled tight to his side, and when Carly had pointedly stared at the woman, Ryman had merely shrugged, turning away.

Heat hit her back at the same time a hand curled around her waist, tugging her sideways. She glanced up to see Neptune wasn't looking at her, but around the clearing at his men. There'd been a minor exodus on foot about thirty minutes ago; then a few minutes ago those same men had returned via the road, riding motorcycles. She'd seen a man with a prospect vest climb off the bike she recognized as Neptune's, that idea reinforced when the man tipped an imaginary hat to his president. The same men had disappeared into the woods a second time, and she suspected they wouldn't be coming back this time.

The sheriff car holding the final killer—Putnam had called them suspects, but she'd relabeled them in her mind—was winding its way down the narrow lane, headed towards the highway and town. The first killer and the traitorous texter she'd told Neptune and Putnam about during the debrief were already on their way to the lockup. The traitor'd been taken in bare from the waist up; Neptune had stripped the vest from his back before the staties had cuffed him. The look on Neptune's face had been murderous as he'd folded and refolded the vest, gaze locked on the man who'd betrayed his club for a thin wad of bills. The van she and the other two women had been abducted in was in the process of being loaded onto a wrecker, and the cluster of police had dwindled down to just a couple.

"I think we're fuckin' finally free to go." Neptune's voice rumbled next to her ear as pleasant shivers chased across her skin at the sound. "You up for another ride, Carly?"

Before she could answer, Putnam walked up, hand shading his eyes against the floodlights brought in to illuminate the scene. "Dobbs." He thrust his hand out as he greeted them, and Neptune adjusted his hold on her to accept it, shaking up and down twice before releasing. "Gibson." The hand was thrust at her and she nearly missed her cue, so surprised that he'd treat her just like he had the man standing at her back. She gripped Putnam's hand, tightening around his fingers and offering the same double shake Neptune had. "I think we've got everything we need, but don't be surprised if you get a call from the prosecutor.

He's gonna have a field day with this one." He paused and shook his head but didn't seem to expect a response, because he continued talking. "Glad it's handled and done in a way that gives us all closure." That seemed to be aimed at Neptune, and when she glanced up at him, he was glaring back at Putnam.

"Just keep him locked up this time." Neptune's words hit Putnam hard, and the cop blanched as he nodded. "Stay safe, Putnam."

"Will do." The state cop turned and took a few steps away before he paused and looked back, gaze fixed on her. "You stickin' around, Gibson?"

"Maybe." That was all she was willing to offer him, and he clearly understood, giving her a single slow nod before he continued on his way. She decided to address the exchange in a sideways manner that allowed her and Neptune to move past it. "That was weird." Neptune huffed a humorless laugh. "It was."

"Yeah, it was. Let's get in the wind, Carly." He wrapped a hand around hers, fingers threading through as he gave her a tug. "Come on."

She stood next to his bike, chin lifted as he fit the helmet on her. It seemed a thousand years since he'd performed the task for the first time, not a span of time measured in hours. He called out a goodbye as she settled onto the seat behind him, and at the first movement of the bike beneath them, she leaned forwards and wrapped her hands around his waist. It was the easiest thing in the world to relax and trust him to get them to the highway safely, no matter the road was rock and sand, and then once on the highway, to maintain her deeply relaxed state. Being a passive passenger wasn't high on her list of things she would have thought she'd like, but based on her body's response to being on the bike with this man, she'd have been wrong.

She didn't think she'd dozed off, but she'd certainly tuned out to an extent, because it surprised her when the bike slowed to a crawl as Neptune pulled into the driveway of a house. In the dark, it was hard to pick out details, but she could see it appeared neatly maintained. About what she'd expect for an ex-military guy who was big on control.

Climbing off the bike, she stood nearby as he parked it, handing him the helmet when he finished. Suddenly struck by nerves she didn't understand, she fumbled for words. "Neptune, I'm not sure—"

"Just come inside, Carly. I'm beat, too. Let's get some rest, yeah?" He cut her off, then blew out a heavy sigh.

She studied him for a moment, then dipped her chin once in a nod of agreement. There was no arguing what he'd stated clearly. She was exhausted and even more emotionally wrung out. Finding herself in the place where her father had been killed, with his murderers at her mercy, it had been all she could do to step back and allow the law to rule.

"Hey." Neptune's quiet voice was closer than it had been, and Carly realized her eyes had closed without her permission. "Let's get inside. You look just as tired as I feel."

"I am." She accepted his outstretched hand, smiling as he threaded their fingers as he'd done earlier. There was a casual intimacy to that action she found she liked. A lot. She deliberately set aside that feeling, deciding to just accept instead of defining for once.

Following him through the garage and into the house was easy, something done on autopilot, but once inside, she'd balked when he'd stopped in front of a bedroom that was clearly not his. She resisted his attempt to steer her inside, and looking up at his face, she saw hunger there. That gave her the confidence to argue with him, because she knew the guest room wasn't due to a lack of desire, but just the goodness in him coming out in yet another way. "No, not here. I want to be with you."

There was a long moment of silence when she wasn't sure if he'd agree or banish her to the purgatory of the guest room anyway. Finally he stepped backwards, a single stride as he tugged on her hand. When she went with him willingly, he wordlessly led her farther along the hallway and into a darkened room. Pulling her to a spot alongside the massive bed, he dropped her hand, retreating. A moment later, she heard a muted click, and limited light flowed into the room through a doorway leading to what looked like a bathroom. A rustling came from somewhere along the wall, and he came back to her with a piece of fabric bundled into his fist. He thrust it at her and she took it, letting it unfold to see it was a tee. Large as it was, it had to be his, and Carly felt a tiny sense of satisfaction that she'd be sleeping in his shirt.

"Bathroom's in there. I don't have any spare toothbrushes, but there's toothpaste in the cabinet. Water heats up fast, and I got a big tank, so you soak as long as you need to." He stepped away, intent on heading to the hall, but he paused in the doorway. Looking back at her with an inscrutable expression, Neptune told her, "I'm gonna make us something quick to eat. You gotta be hungry. I'll be back in a few minutes, but you take your time, yeah?" She nodded, and he watched her, gaze fixed on her face. "So fuckin' glad you're okay. Glad you're safe. Glad you're here." Fingers rapping out a quick double tap against the doorframe, he turned and left.

Carly didn't snoop, didn't spend any time scoping out his bedroom. She beelined for the bathroom and had the shower running hot in only a couple of minutes. She studied herself in the mirror for the briefest of moments, surprised at the eagerness on the face of the woman she saw there. Something about his declaration in that clearing had not just struck a chord inside her but had swept in like a tidal wave, filling her up.

His words repeated, falling from her lips as she remembered the vulnerable look on his face as he'd asked, "You gonna save me?" Whirling away from her image, she stripped efficiently and stepped under the pounding water, lifting her face to the welcome wet and heat. *Maybe I will.*

Nine

Neptune

Arms braced against the counter, he stared at the dark window, the glass reflecting a blurry image of him and the room. He wasn't regretting the decision to leave the fate of those two assholes up to Carly, not exactly, but he was feeling the effects of having so much adrenaline rushing through his system for so long and no good outlet. Unreasonable anger still stirred in his gut, a desire to have put everything to ground tonight. Second-guessing himself wasn't something he did often, and he wasn't happy his mind had picked right now to start.

He had to admit it had felt right in a lot of ways to climb on his bike with Carly sitting behind him, rolling away from the clearing in the woods with both of them unharmed and—more than anything else—together. She hadn't questioned his need to hold her or have his hands on her at any point, and when he'd attempted to put a pause on things by parking her in the guest bedroom, she'd made it very clear where she expected to spend the night.

He just had to get a grip on himself so he didn't fuck this up.

Movement in the reflection warned him of her entry into the room, so he didn't jump when she spoke. "I thought you were going to make food?"

"You hungry?" Throat tight, he had to force the words out. Even just via the blurred image, the sight of her in his shirt pulled the already taut spring inside him even tighter. Much more and he felt like he'd explode. "I've got sandwich stuff." She'd moved as he was speaking, her likeness finally disappearing behind his. A moment later, her arms slid around his waist as she pressed herself tight to his back. "Shower work okay?"

"Yeah, the shower was great." She gave him a squeeze; then he lost the heat of her body against his. An instant later, she'd wedged herself in front of him, caging herself between his arms. He looked down as she settled her cheek against his chest, arms encircling his waist again. "I'm not really hungry, no. More tired than anything." She sighed as he straightened, wrapping both arms around her, one hand cradling her head. "This is nice, Neptune."

"It's Angelo, actually. I mean, you can call me Neptune if you want, but I think I'd like it if you called me Angelo." From this angle, he could just see the curve of her cheek lift and knew she was smiling. "What?"

"Angel." He froze at the word, overcome with the need to dispute that nickname, far removed from the man he'd been for so very long. Then she gave him a squeeze and whispered, "I like it," and he relaxed slightly.

"What do you want from me tonight, Carly?" She stilled in his arms, and for an instant, he wondered if he'd asked the wrong question. Whatever she put to words, even if it was that damned guest room instead of his bed, he'd make it happen for her. *She's worth so much more*, he thought.

"I want whatever you want." Her laughter was quick and light as she pulled back and lifted her eyes so she could see his face. "I don't think I've ever said that to a man before. I'm generally very specific when it comes to things like being in bed, but tonight's thrown me for a loop. I..." Her voice trailed off for a moment. "I'm tired, Angel. Tired and sad, and still kinda turned on. Can we just see where this goes tonight?"

"I can do that. For you." He gave her a squeeze and turned, hauling her against his side as he moved them towards the bedroom. "For you, I can do anything."

He stripped to his underwear and flung the covers back, sprawling across the middle of the mattress. She followed him between the sheets, curling close to his side as she slung an arm across his gut. As she had everywhere else, she fit against him perfectly. Carly sighed deeply as she nestled her head on his shoulder, the slide of her hair on his skin a sweet tease that had his cock chubbing up, fingers tingling as blood rushed to his groin. Her hand gliding along his side had his abs tightening in response, his cock jerking and uncurling at his hip.

"Baby, if you wanna sleep, you're gonna have to keep your hands still." One arm around her back, he had a hand draped over her hip and dug his fingers in slightly for emphasis. Neptune lifted his other hand and caressed her cheek before slipping his fingers through her hair. Eyes closed, he continued to pet her, and she sagged against him, her muscles giving up most of the tension she'd carried all through their ride home.

When she finally spoke, they'd been quiet for so long her voice startled him. "And if I don't wanna sleep yet?"

With a grin, Neptune arched his back, jutting his hips up in response to the continued roving of her hand. She laughed quietly at his antics, but her hand dipped south as he'd hoped. He hadn't expected her to be a passive partner in bed, and this underscored how right he'd been. It also gave him a chance to learn just a little more about Carly, something he was coming to find he wanted more than he'd expected. Wanted to know all about her. Fingertips traced along the edge of his waistband, and he let her know how that felt with a soft groan and another shift of his hips.

"Then you just keep on doin' what you're doin', and we'll be up for a while yet."

Her fingertips pushed past the fabric and curled around the crown of his cock. Quick heat and pressure, a gentle tug at the head before those clever fingers trailed along the shaft to the root. He'd gotten rock hard at her touch, his cock arching away from his body, creating a tent within his boxer briefs that gave her easy access to him. She took advantage, jacking him with a loose grip for a few moments before she abandoned his cock to explore his sac and balls. As she gently rolled and caressed, he shifted his grip on her hip, moving to cup her ass, digging his fingers in as he pulled her against his hip.

"I'd say you were already up." A firm stroke accompanied her teasing words, and he groaned, twisting to face her. Knuckle under her chin, he lifted her face to fit his mouth over hers. He skimmed his fingers down her side, finding and slipping underneath the hem of the tee she wore. The remembered pleasure of seeing her in his shirt swept over him. As he teased her lips with the tip of his tongue, his fingertips followed the contours of her body up and up, over her ribs until he palmed a bare breast. Her nipple pebbled underneath his hand as his tongue dipped into her mouth, stroking and tasting.

"Oh, yeah." Nipping and plucking at her bottom lip, he kissed her softly. "With you playin' around like this, I'm always gonna be up for you." Deepening the kiss, he teased her with touches timed to the thrust of his tongue until she clamped down on his bottom lip. *"Fuck."* He pulled his lip from between her teeth, the sting of the pinch making his dick jump in her hand. "You're pokin' the bear, baby. You sure you want this tonight?" He thrust against her, fucking her fist with a slow, deliberate rhythm. "I'll take everything you wanna give me, but I warn you, I'm an advantage-taker. You give me an inch"—finger and thumb met at her nipple, giving it a hard tweak that made her mewl sweetly—"I'm gonna take a mile." He curved his other arm down, hand slipping between her legs and stroking across her core, heat building in his gut to find her already wet. "Fuckin' drenched for me. Love that. Fuckin' love it." She squirmed under his attention, and he rolled her to her back, covering her and slipping between her thighs when she spread her legs, inviting him in.

With an arm on either side of her, he pushed up in the bed, grinding his erection against her. Carly's hands rested on his hips, fingers holding tight as he stared down at her. "You want this, baby?"

Her lids dipped closed, and he was startled to see a single tear slip from the corner of her eye, gliding across her temple and dampening her hair. *Fuck, I got it wrong.* He was quickly adjusting, already about to slide off her when her hands clamped down, holding him in place.

"No, that's not—" Her laughter was broken, filled with tears, and he tensed again, cautiously trying to gently break her grip. "Angel"—that name, so wrong only a few moments ago, now felt like benediction against his skin—"stay, please. It's not you, promise. I want this."

"Coulda fooled me." Studying her with narrowed eyes, he saw the flash of annoyance she had at his words. He pushed forwards, wanting her to understand what it looked like from where he was. "Woman cries when I get between her legs, that doesn't say she's into it at all. Person's been through what you've been through over the past few days, it's no harm and no foul if I got it wrong. Long as I didn't hurt you. If I did, that'd be unforgivable." The idea of taking advantage of her during a moment of weakness turned his stomach. Bitter acid churned in his gut. "Yes is only yes until it's not. Either side of this equation gets to call a timeout if needed."

"You're beautiful, you know that?" As she spoke, Carly's eyes flew open, and he saw more wet swimming there, causing him to renew his efforts to extricate himself from her hands. "Please, Angelo. Please, just give me a minute here." At her use of his name, he stilled, waiting. "You're perfect, and I wish I could just do this without telling you everything, but this—" Her fingers tightened painfully for an instant before releasing, her palms sliding up his back and pulling him down against her. "This matters to me. I won't have it start with lies between us." She smiled up at him, a there and gone expression that gave him hope enough to believe her words for now. "I'd rather it not start with anything between us." Her pointed glance down at the shirt she wore explained her statement, and he chuckled softly, letting the sound die away as he realized she wasn't done talking. Carly swallowed hard, the words still coming, but slowly and with visible pain. "But I *need* you to understand before it goes that far. Before it goes any further. It's selfish, I know. So selfish, but I like you where you are right now, and it'd help if you stayed with me for a while. Let me get through this."

"I can do that for you, Carly. I told you…" He dipped closer and pressed a soft kiss against the tip of her nose. "Whatever you need."

"Right now, I need this."

Neptune let his weight settle against her, pinning her to the mattress as he planted a forearm next to her head. Leaning against his hand, he stared at her for a moment, then gave it to her again, willing to do it as many times as it took for it to sink in that he was serious. "You got it, doll."

***

Carly

Something Ryman had said today had stuck with her, and she held to his words as she fought to bring her whirling thoughts under control. *"He already looks at you like you're his world."* That had been right after the memorial ride ended, in those moments when she'd been so raw and humbled she'd needed to find a place to be alone for a few minutes, just to pull herself together. She hadn't asked him what he'd meant, but looking up at Angelo Dobbs, aka Neptune, she thought she understood.

Please, God, she prayed, feeling like it was another foxhole plea, alike and yet dissimilar from the thousands she'd lifted up over the years.

"My mom had a sister. She was younger than Mom, only a couple years older than me. When my grandparents passed, she came to live with us. I remember my friends in school thinking it funny that I called her Aunt Jan, because she was a high school senior while I was a freshman." She swallowed hard, trying to find room in her throat for the words she needed to say. "Aunt Jan went to college out of state, and the fifth week of the first semester, she dropped off the surface of the earth. Daddy turned over every leaf and stone, talked to cops there in Virginia, and came up empty. They kept telling him it was a good-girl-gone-bad scenario, but he and I knew differently."

When she paused for a breath, Angel traced her jaw with his finger, hand settling on her throat in a comforting gesture she needed. "They never found her, but Daddy had a friend who'd heard about a guy recruiting at her campus." She shook her head. "And by recruiting, I mean abducting girls and boys and sending them to training camps, where they'd come out with a specific set of skills and a monkey on their back."

"You ever get a name for that recruiter?" The man staring at her now wasn't Angel, not even Neptune. This was Dobbs, the military man she suspected had a lock on where she was going with her story.

"Yeah. Name and then another name, and a short list of contacts. I was out of school by then, attending the academy. Daddy wouldn't let me in on anything he was doing, but he kept me up to date on what was going down."

"Good man, trying to do right by his girls."

"Yeah, I know. It pissed me off at the time, but I understand. So fast forward to my career. I used to work for DOJ. I wasn't able to get what I needed from that route, so I got away from that and went to work for a private company. They've got operatives in all different kinds of specialties. There's a lot I can't tell you, but they can infiltrate businesses, agencies, countries—hell, even families if needed." Angel—and didn't she just love that name, letting it roll around inside her head, spreading light and sparkling hope everywhere it went—stared down at her with a carefully neutral expression. Neither encouraging nor discouraging. She didn't realize it was what she needed to get through this until he'd donned the expression. "I've taken lots of jobs over the past few years. Daddy knew some of it, but he wasn't happy about me leaving the government job. Not after working my way up through the ranks and into the pocket of the general who set me up at the DOJ."

When she paused there, he didn't urge her to continue, didn't give her any indication he was impatient for her to get past this need to flay herself in front of him before they slept together for the first time. *First of many*, she hoped, momentarily crossing her fingers.

"I was looking for anyone with a connection to the names I had. Those were the jobs that appealed, ones where I could put another pin in the wall of information, or where I could take an operation down. Ones that resembled what I knew Aunt Jan had been initiated into. Some of the jobs required I put myself into situations that shouldn't have happened. I did it, but these weren't anything close to usual, you know?" As soon as she asked the question, she shook her head and scoffed far back in her throat. "Of course you don't know; that's why I'm telling you. Sorry."

"Don't be sorry, baby. This is hard. I can see that just from your expression." He smoothed her hair back from her face, the touch infinitely tender and caring, and she turned her face into his hand, pressing a kiss to his palm. "Before you go on, I want you to hear me. Really, really hear me."

Carly stared up at him, waiting. His gaze moved over her face, but he held his silence until she nodded slowly.

"I got a feeling I know what's coming, and while I hate that for you, it doesn't matter to me. Nothing that happened before you walked in that kitchen a couple nights ago matters. Anything that you did or was done to you—all that pales by the perfection of you right here in my bed, in my arms. You need to tell me, I'll listen, but in the end, it won't factor in what happens between us." As he spoke, his thumb stroked along her cheekbone, a simple back and forth that anchored her. "I'm sorry you lost your aunt that way. I get what drove you, Carly girl. I totally get it. I was in the military, and I don't talk about it much, but my job was killing people. Not usually from far away, although I did that too. My job was to get up close and take my targets out while they were in impossible situations, which meant the path to them was never clear. I worked through the shadows or in the crush of a crowd, but the end result was I did my job. I did it and was good at my job. But that's no longer my job." He lifted one shoulder, bending close enough to brush the tip of her nose with his in a caress as sweet as his touch on her face. "I don't give a flying fuck what you did for the DOJ or that private outfit you work for. I only care about you."

"You make it sound so easy."

"It's as easy as you let it be, honey. You want it to be hard, want to tear yourself up about how I'm going to react? Well, don't. Because I won't. You'll get no recriminations from me." He brought his mouth closer, and she lifted up to meet him halfway, pressing her lips to his in an eyes-wide-open, trembling kiss. The steely resolve in his gaze reassured her that he really did mean everything he was saying, and he reiterated it when they separated finally. "Easy as you let it be. Be easy, baby. Be easy."

"The last job was one of those trafficking rings. We broke it up, saved nearly a hundred women and girls this time. Lost a bunch of them who were too far gone, but we saved so many. Got records on the movers and shakers in that world, and I matched things to the man. I got him,

Angel. We got him and it's over. It can be over, if I want it to be. My boss has suggested that be my last job for a while." Her breath caught in her chest at the remembered shadow world where she'd lived for so long. "It was so bad, Angel. And to get inside, to earn my way in, I had to—"

"I've got a better idea than you think what it took to earn your way inside." He bent his neck, putting his face close to hers again. Speaking slowly, enunciating clearly with pauses between each word, he told her, "I. Don't. Care."

Can it really be that easy for him? She blinked and, for an instant, was back in that tiny cell where her every move was watched, where she was fodder for fantasy for so many men, where so many evil acts had happened. Another blink and all she could see was Angel, right there in front of her. *Easy as I let it be*, she reminded herself, and felt the corners of her lips curl in a tiny smile.

Rocking her hips up against him, she got to see his mouth fall open in surprise. Had a front-row seat to witness the hunger stir back to life in his eyes as he sucked his bottom lip into his mouth on a low grunt. "God, baby." As if her action had given him permission to move, and she supposed it had, he ground down against her. His erection had flagged while they talked, which meant she now got to feel it coming back to life, hardening against her as he thrust in a slow, rolling motion.

"Make love to me." Carly ran her hands up his arms and over his shoulders, trailing the hard edges of her nails against his back until she gripped the globes of his ass. "Please, Angel?" She pulled and lifted at the same moment, firming the contact between their bodies from breasts to knees.

"My baby don't gotta beg me." His head fell, and his mouth covered hers in a voracious kiss that went on and on. The muscles in his ass bunched under her hands as he moved over her, and Carly was on the edge in only moments, her breath coming ragged and quick against his lips. "Not sayin' I don't like it, 'cause I surely do."

"Please?" She kissed him softly, tongue dipping between his lips to explore and taste. "Please?" This was a murmur against his cheek as she trailed a line of gentle kisses along his jaw. He groaned when she reached his ear and breathed another plea. "Please, Angel?"

***

Neptune

Soft and giving in his arms, Carly had clearly put aside the need to bare her soul to him, and he hoped it wasn't just in response to his disclaimers but because of them. There'd be a difference and he'd know it over the upcoming days and weeks. If she returned to the topic out of a misplaced need to give him an out of having a relationship with her, he'd do his best to set her right again.

His earlier exhaustion had fled, and now he was buoyed up on a soaring need to be inside her, to feel her around him, under him, to work his way under her skin as she'd surely done to him. The remembered terror from the events of the evening tried to creep in, but he squashed those.

Knowing even more about Carly's skill set now, just from the tiny amount he'd gotten from her, he knew he'd have to come to grips with the fact his woman could hold her own in situations like that. He'd had more than one conversation with Wolf on the same topic as the man had wrapped his head around how competent Rose was, because it meant his inner caveman wasn't needed as much as Wolf wanted to be. The couple had finally come to a balanced cooperative arrangement, and Neptune trusted he and Carly would do the same. *Bank on it*, he thought, holding tight to the thought that she'd be around long enough so he could watch it happen.

Her teeth latched on to his earlobe, and he tightened his grip on her, sliding his hips back and forth in a writhing circle that targeted her core. The groan she gave him was worth the ache in his cock at the firm pressure, and he fell into a rocking movement against her. Mouth on her throat, he kissed his way down to the delicate lines of her collarbones, nudging the fabric of the shirt she wore aside to reach more of her soft skin.

"Lose the shirt, baby." He was already tired of fighting the garment, and he pushed up so he was propped over her at arm's length. "Love seein' you in my tee, but I'm over it. Wanna see you in the altogether, which is nothin' at all."

The smile she gave him was blindingly bright, carrying a fond affection that felt more profound than the desire in her eyes. She gave him back the words spoken earlier in the evening. "You got it, Angel."

Her hands moved between them, but instead of bringing the shirt over her head, she worked at the waistband of his underwear, and he lifted as she shoved the material down over his ass, halfway down his thighs. His rigid cock bounced free, slapping against his belly before arcing in an eager curve away from his body. Pushing to his knees, he finished removing boxers as he watched her graceful movements that swept free of her body not only the shirt but also the tiny scrap between her legs until she was naked, laid out before him.

Mesmerized by the sight, he followed the path of her fingers with his gaze as she trailed a soft touch across a scar on her side, another one high on her chest, moving from place to place on her body. It took a moment, but he realized this was Carly showing him her uncertainty. Drawing attention to everything she didn't like on her body would ensure those places were seen.

"Perfect imperfection." Neptune bent and placed a gentle kiss against a scar just above her hip. He repeated the path her fingers had drawn, mouth moving up her body until he was stretched out over her again, nestled between her legs as he held himself up and off her, connected at the hip. "Nothing I'm seein' is gonna put me off you, Carly. I'll want to hear the stories someday, and we can trade tales, because I've got the same records of war written on my skin. Right now? Ah, *God*. Right now, all I wanna do is love you. Gonna let me?"

"Yes." Her hands landed against his flanks, gripping and pulling him tight against her. "Oh, yes."

Staring down, he watched a smile begin to curve her lips and couldn't wait to taste her another minute. Neptune possessed her mouth, falling into the kiss like a man starved, working across her lips once, then a second time. He rolled his hips, thrusting against her, and when her lips parted as his cock glided up and across her clit, he plunged inside her mouth, tongue stroking and twisting with hers.

She wasn't passive, not at all. Carly gave it back to him in equal measures, and he set up a steady rhythm, body and mouth working in a synchronized attack against her senses. She had her own campaign as her hands ran up and down his back, nails threatening one moment, palms soothing the tiny scrapes the next.

"Beautiful." Elbow to the mattress, he propped up on one arm as he slipped his fingers along her side, finding and cupping her breast in his palm. She arched up against him when he tweaked her hardened nipple, her parted lips and the inrush of air evidence of a silent reaction. Her hips moved with greater urgency, legs shifting restlessly as his cock glided through the slick between her pussy lips. "Carly, baby. I wanna be inside you when you come."

"Mmhmm." Eyes closed, she hummed an answer, chin lifted as she thrust her head back when he ground down against her clit. "Please?"

"Oh, yeah." He gave her his weight as he reached across the bed to the drawer of the nightstand. Wrapper in hand, he used fingers and teeth to open the package, rolling the condom on without separating from her any more than absolutely necessary. "My baby don't gotta beg."

Her legs lifted at the same time he rocked his hips back, and the head of his cock notched neatly into her entrance. Neptune pushed forwards, driving into her by a few inches, then held still as she lifted against him, letting her fuck herself, taking him deeper and deeper until he couldn't stand it another moment. Back bowing, he pulled out nearly all the way, then slipped back, pulsing in and out slightly as he forced himself farther inside, grinding against her when he was finally buried to the root.

Her legs folded across his thighs, heels locking right below his ass, and she cried out as she arched up against him again, the name she'd gifted him with buried in the sounds pouring from her throat. "Please, Angel."

Then it was all bets off as he moved over her, inside her, any caution he'd still had thrown to the wind. He couldn't get close enough to her, needed to be with her in a way she'd never lose him, so he'd never lose her. Face buried against her shoulder, he fucked her slowly, using long, deep strokes, twisting his hips when he was balls deep, torturing her clit with every thrust against her body. Sweat slicked both their bodies, and he licked and sucked at her skin, taking in the taste of her there, too.

Carly's fingers threaded through the hair on both sides of his head, and she gripped, lifting him up. She stared up at him, the sight of her wide pupils showing him where she was with their lovemaking. "Wanna see you," she whispered, her chin lifting as he bottomed out again, following through with the roll of his hips that brought the root of his cock into firm contact against her clit. "Angel, I'm gonna come." Her tongue lapped at her lips, and he dipped close enough to brush a kiss across her mouth, but she used the grip she had in his hair to haul him up again. "Wanna see you."

Neptune shoved an arm underneath her back, pushing his hand down to fit his fingers around her ass and lift. The change in angle allowed for even deeper penetration and minutes later gave him a glorious show as she shattered underneath him. Mouth wide in a silent cry, she kept her gaze on his, letting him see every emotion and feeling as she rode the wave up and up, cresting as he crashed their bodies together fierce and fast. He kept up the pace, hammering into her as the orgasm drew out, Carly coming hard as her muscles clenched around his dick.

The lightning that had been coiling at the base of his spine stretched as sounds of his body slapping against hers rose to a frantic pace. "Carly, baby." The tingle curled around the base of his dick, then rushed down his legs and up his spine. He stiffened and thrust deep, deeper as her hold on his head slipped and he bent his neck to kiss her, needing to taste her again, driven to feel her everywhere. Tight heat surrounded him, her arms and legs wrapped wherever she could get a grip, mouths pressed together, his cock pulsing inside her, filling the condom with what felt like molten liquid.

Blissed out, he tore free from her hold on his head and buried his face into the crook of her neck. He stayed like that for a while, holding the bulk of his weight off her as his body trembled with every round of aftershocks that swelled through him, peaking fast and fading slowly. She was responsive even to that, holding tighter and shivering along with him.

"What's your middle name?" Grinning when Carly laughed in surprise at the out-of-the-blue question, he pulled back so he could look into her face. Knuckles to her cheek, he stroked her skin slowly, gently, savoring the contact between them everywhere.

"Jane." She wrinkled her nose. "Carly Jane. I can still hear my mom yelling for me across the base housing. Where'd Neptune come from?"

Ignoring her question for now, he asked something he already knew. "Gibby was still enlisted when she passed, right?" When Neptune moved to pull out, Carly's arms and legs tightened and she moaned softly. He smiled and leaned down to trace the line of her cheekbone with the tip of his nose. Mouth close to her ear, he whispered, "Baby, gotta take care of the condom."

"I know."

The grumbling tone made him grin. When he pulled back to smile at her, Carly snapped her teeth at him, prompting him to possess her mouth again. The sliding glide of tongues and soft caress of her lips against his was heaven revisited.

"Carly Jane, I gotta take care of the condom, baby." The movement of her mouth under his telegraphed her contented smile.

"I never liked my middle name before this exact instant." Fingers fisting in his hair, she drew him down for another soft kiss, then gave his shoulder a gentle shove. "Okay, fine. Go take care of business."

"Hey, Carly?" He called her name like a question and waited for her gaze to return to his face. "Fair warning, I'm the kinda guy who's all-in on things he likes."

A tiny frown drew her brows together. "Okay?"

"I like you." Neptune gave her the words while on the move, rolling off while gripping the condom to his softening cock. Removing the used rubber, he swung his legs over the edge of the bed and jackknifed to standing, then looked over his shoulder at her as he walked to the bathroom. "Be prepared."

"Prepared for what?"

The confusion in her voice was reflected on her face, and he paused, staring at her for a moment before he continued out of the room, losing sight of her as he called back, "Everything."

LACK OF IN-BETWEEN

Ten

Neptune

"You're a hell of a president, Neptune."

"Appreciate the confidence, brother." He grinned at Blade and lifted his beer slightly in an acknowledging salute. His other hand was otherwise occupied, curled around Carly's hip to hold her against his side. She was busily chatting with Amanda, one palm pressed to the side of the woman's tiny baby belly. Her other arm was trapped under his across their backs, her fingers curled into his back pocket.

Scanning the room inside the clubhouse, he saw the face of every member present, along with some trusted guests. The event was a baby shower the women had organized for Amanda and Monk, gifting the couple with all the necessary and unnecessary—in Neptune's eyes—things for bringing a baby home from the hospital.

Carly had been wrapping gifts a couple of nights ago, and he'd watched with amusement as she'd taped the pastel-colored paper over no less than four boxes filled with diapers and wipes. When he'd asked about the quantity, she'd rolled her eyes at him and pointed out they were different sizes, claiming it wasn't something new parents thought about as they were dealing with caring for a tiny newborn. That had been followed by a half a dozen more boxes with blankets and outfits.

She'd ceased holding up each item for his approval when he'd likened something called a sleep sack to the current male fashion craze of rompers, begging her in a high voice for a sleep sack of his very own. Her pique hadn't lasted long, only until he'd thrown himself onto the floor beside her and caught her in his arms, rolling so she was on top of him, chin propped on her wrists and staring down at him.

His heart clenched at their remembered conversation, but not painfully.

"I want to stay here."

He froze at the meaning behind the whispered words, then shoved his hands under her arms, yanking her up his body so he could reach her lips. This was in response to his reaction a week ago when Ryman had called with a job.

She'd turned it down, but only after giving it serious consideration, and the fear that had gripped him had come out as misdirected anger. Thank God she'd recognized it as such, not taking his clipped responses and the constant refrain of slammed doors and cabinets as a personal slight. He'd known their time together would be dictated by her work, but knowing and accepting were two very different things. Her telling him this now meant she'd come to a decision.

"I want you here always." Arms banded around her back, he held her in place, not that she was trying to disengage. Carly's body lay on top of his, relaxed even as he hauled her around like he had. "Always, you fuckin' hear me?"

"I hear you, Angel. I've been hearing you from the beginning." She shook her head slowly, hair cascading and shifting around her face as she stared down at him, her gaze intense. "I don't know what this means for me long-term, but for now, I've taken myself out of rotation for jobs."

"Means I get to keep you. Right fuckin' here." He gave her a squeeze, holding until she pretended to gasp for breath. "Right here."

"I'm going to have to find work. I can't just sit around."

"Wolf's looking for someone to help at the garage. Wants someone who's willing to help him plot out bigger builds. A strategic role, not wrenching on bikes. More about

thinking and planning." He offered up the first thing that came to mind, warmth spreading through him as her face softened. "Rose said the staties are always looking for good people to bring into the local troop. I know a guy over in Birmingham who has a raft of PIs on his payroll, if you wanted to get a license to practice. There's a thousand opportunities at your fingertips."

"Sounds like you've been planning for this possibility." She dipped her mouth to press against his, touching their lips together in a soft series of kisses. "I love that you thought about me like this."

"Wanna keep you. Wanted that since I met you." He caressed her cheek with the backs of his bent fingers, stroking slowly across her skin. "Been waitin' on the chance you'd want it too."

"Carly Jane." He waited, and she gave him what he wanted, that bright smile aimed in his direction, gaze locked to his with a questioning arch of one eyebrow. "Love you, woman."

Neptune got to see that sink in, the meaning of his words hitting her as she turned away from Amanda, hand lifting to rest against his chest. "Oh yeah?" The soft question was followed by the tiniest quiver of her lips, and he tilted his head, bringing his mouth down to cover hers in a long, slow, deep, wet, entirely possessive kiss.

He drew her closer, their embrace turning into a slow dance as he shuffled them in a small circle and Carly's head rested against his shoulder, face turned into his neck. Her lips stroked across his skin in a series of sweet touches.

"Oh yeah."

LACK OF IN-BETWEEN

Epilogue

Neptune

Neptune lifted a fist, then pointed before turning on his indicator. He watched in the mirror as the line of bikes inchwormed together, slowing and readying for the upcoming turn. The lot wasn't huge, but he knew from experience over the past couple of years that it would be big enough. He made his accustomed sweeping turn and rolled back towards the entrance in time for Carly's arms to come down on either side of his head. She held the phone in front of them, recording each bike as they rolled into the cemetery parking lot, no need to narrate because each man and woman glanced in their direction, giving their version of a smile or stoic chin lift.

This had become a ritual for the Borderline Freaks MC and their close friends, members of supporting clubs as well as alliances. He'd left it to Monk to organize this year, as he should, their road captain meting out riding assignments according to the personal association with Neptune or Carly first. That meant Ryman was directly behind the BFMC members, ahead of the prospects even. Neptune grinned. He'd been talking to Ryman about moving, coming back to town to stay. But apparently the man had finally met someone over in Birmingham and was loathe to leave the new relationship to the foibles of long distance.

It took minutes during which he pulled up a little farther, angling back into a spot along the edge of the parking lot. By the time all the bikes had entered, each side of the lot was filled, and there was a double line down through the center. Good turnout, and he made a note to say as much to Monk.

Before he could kill the bike, Carly thumbed the camera into selfie mode, kept it aimed on their faces, and smiled big as she blew the camera a kiss.

Next to him, Monk and Amanda were already off their bike, Amanda's belly rounded with their second child. Marty, their oldest at four years old, had stayed back at the clubhouse along with other little ones, watched over by the teenaged kids like Wolf's daughter, Erika.

Carly leaned against him, head resting against his back. She'd gotten home from a gig late last night, Ryman driving them both back from wherever they'd been posted. They'd be headed back out tomorrow, because the job wasn't yet done. Neptune didn't like her working so much, but she'd let him know in no uncertain terms that he didn't get to dictate to her about the pregnancy. "Women have been having babies since time began" was her go-to these days. Not that he could argue the point.

Didn't make him worry less, though.

Amanda murmured something to Monk that made him laugh and wrap his arms around her. Neptune knew they'd go to her husband's grave first and pay their respects. It was their ritual, too.

Wolf strolled up, Rose in the curve of his arm, and Blade followed behind, hand linked with Jenn's.

Time to head up the hill to where three flags stood tall.

One was near Amanda's first husband. Neptune remembered the honor ride the community had held for the man when he was killed overseas. Had ridden in it, flattered to be able to pay his respects in a way that held his fidelity up for all to see. Pride had been thick on his skin that day, something he would give a lot to change. The president role for the Freaks had taught him service was the more profound act, and being humble more attractive.

One flag was near where Frootloop had been laid to rest eight months ago. Neptune and his brothers had carried him to the graveside, eschewing usage of the hearse beyond the edge of the parking lot. It had been a hard climb up the hill, rain whipping sideways and soaking them, but the man had served his country in time of need, and served the Freaks well, too. He deserved no less.

The flag farthest from where they stood was planted within feet of where Gibby lay. They'd raised the stars and stripes on the day his killers had died, stuck like a pig in prison. Neptune suspected Ryman's hands were at the end of the trail leading to that culmination, forestalling a need to go to trial and saving Carly so much grief. Neptune had been poised to make the same call, had picked up the phone and chatted with Retro down in Birmingham, only to be told it was already in motion.

Gibby would have been proud to call Ryman brother, just like Neptune was.

Fingers latched onto his belt loop, and he lifted his arm in invitation. Carly ducked under and curled against his side, her hand slipping across his belly in a gentle caress. The woman had no idea what it did to him when she claimed him like this. He wanted to beat his chest and howl, warning all the males in the area that she was his.

He didn't. Mostly because she wouldn't like it.

Instead, he slipped his hand up the back of her neck, tangled his fingers in her hair, gripped, and angled her head back. Then he swooped down for a kiss.

It was just as sweet as the first had been.

But not as sweet as the next would be.

~~~
~~~

THANK YOU SO MUCH FOR READING
See You in Valhalla!

This story is the fourth and final story in the Borderline Freaks MC series. I'm so pleased you've taken this journey with me and the guys from the BFMC, and I hope you enjoyed it as much as I did.

ABOUT THE AUTHOR

Raised in the south, *Wall Street Journal* & *USA TODAY* bestselling author MariaLisa learned about the magic of books at an early age. Every summer, she would spend hours in the local library, devouring books of every genre. Self-described as a book-a-holic, she says "I've always loved to read, but then I discovered writing, and found I adored that, too. For reading...if nothing else is available, I've been known to read the back of the cereal box."

Want sneak peeks into what she's working on, or to chat with other readers about her books? Join the Facebook group! **bit.ly/deMora-FB-group**

deMora's got a spam-free newsletter list she'd love to have you join, too: **bit.ly/mldemora-newsletter**

~~~~~
~~~~~

Borderline Freaks MC series

This series is comprised of four stories, and are best read in order to avoid spoilery situations.

Service and Sacrifice

"Thank you for your service" is what we're taught to say to military men and women in gratitude for our freedoms won at their expense. Less often do we thank their families, those left behind to hold down the fort, to manage the day-to-day struggle of keeping everything up in the air until their loved one returns.

When you can't count on anyone else to save you, there's only one real choice.

Amanda lost her husband to war. Alex lost part of himself. Through a series of glancing encounters, Amanda and Alex find reasons to continue on. And together, they'll discover hope and peace can be found in the most unexpected of places.

books2read.com/serviceandsacrifice

~~~

More Than Enough

When a man sees himself as damaged, imperfect, and flawed, it's hard to believe there could be love in his future. After a near-fatal accident stripped Blade of his confidence, he didn't hold out much hope ... for anything.
~~~

Until Jenn—gorgeous, sweet, and kind—dropped into his life.

Where he sees destruction, she sees perfection.

Where he sees helplessness, she sees courage.

Where he sees ruin, she sees strength.

Can he ever believe he's more than enough?

books2read.com/morethanenough

~~~

Lack of In-between

Wolf finds Rose harbors more secrets than he expected, and the deeper he pulls her into his life, the more he likes it.

Once a man's been embedded in the bloody aftermath of battle after battle, with no relief in sight, he's forever changed.

Wolf came home from overseas to find his world askew. He was no longer a husband, since he and his ex agreed they were better friends than partners. But he still held the coveted position of father, an experience so confusing and rewarding it sometimes left him breathless.
~~~

He's got a lot on his plate personally, and even more with the Borderline Freaks and the challenges he and his club brothers have hit lately.

He just doesn't have time to make room for a relationship.

Right?

books2read.com/lackofinbetween

~~~

See You in Valhalla

This is Angelo Dobbs' worst nightmare. A good man lies dead, and with the Borderline Freaks MC's president and founding member gone, the leadership position within the club falls to him.

It's not that he can't manage the easy task of leading a group of good men; he would just have preferred to stay a little farther out of the spotlight. But when his brothers issue the call, he answers.

Carly Gibson, daughter of his dead friend, is an unexpected—but not unwelcome—complication for his new role. She's the most intriguing woman he's ever met, capable and filled with a strength of character. He finds himself instinctively drawn to her. Could he have found the woman meant to complete him, finally?
~~~

Over the past couple of years, Dobbs—Neptune to the men of the BFMC—has watched as his closest friends found their soulmates. Now, their women are an integral part of the club. When they and Carly are threatened, Neptune will do anything to ensure their safety—and, just maybe, his future.

books2read.com/seeyouinvalhalla

Other Motorcycle Club Romance Series

My Rebel Wayfarers MC and the Neither This Nor That MC series do cross over, along with the Occupy Yourself band books, so readers have a couple of choices. The series can be read independently beginning with RWMC, OYBS, and then NTNT without too many spoilers. There's also a crossover between my RWMC world and Lila Rose's Hawks MC world. Or they can be read intertwined—in chronological order.

Here's the recommended reading order if you want to follow according to timing:

Mica, RWMC #1

A Sweet & Merry Christmas, RWMC #1.5

Slate, RWMC #2

Bear, RWMC #3

Born Into Trouble, OYBS #1

Jase, RWMC #4

Gunny, RWMC #5

Mason, RWMC #6

Hoss, RWMC #7

This Is the Route of Twisted Pain, NTNT #1

Harddrive Holidays, RWMC #7.5

Duck, RWMC #8

Biker Chick Campout, RWMC #8.5

Watcher, RWMC #9

Treading the Traitor's Path: Out Bad, NTNT #2

Living Without, Lila Rose's Hawks MC: Caroline Springs #4

Shelter My Heart, NTNT #3

A Kiss to Keep You, RWMC #9.25

Gun Totin' Annie, RWMC #9.5

Secret Santa, RWMC #9.75

Trapped by Fate on Reckless Roads, NTNT #4

Bones, RWMC #10

Gunny's Pups, RWMC #10.25

Not Even A Mouse, RWMC #10.75

Road Runner's Ride, RWMC #12.5

Never Settle, RWMC #10.5

Fury, RWMC #11

Christmas Doings, RWMC #11.25

Gypsy's Lady, RWMC #11.5

Thunderstruck, NTNT #5

Going Down Easy

No Man's Land

Cassie, RWMC #12

~~~~~
~~~~~

Also by MariaLisa deMora

Neither This Nor That MC romance series

Legends are born from moments like these. Folktales spun around a single point in time so perfect, you can almost hear the click resonating through the universe as things align. Meet Twisted, Po'Boy, Retro, and Ragman, good old boys from southern states who have many things in common. First, is a bone-deep love of the biker lifestyle. Second, would be their love of the brotherhood, and knowing that you trust the man at your back. Finally, these men have the love of a good woman. None of these come without a price, and it is our pleasure to journey along with them as they discover the blessings that can be won, and lost along the way.

This is the Route of Twisted Pain
Treading the Traitor's Path: Out Bad
Shelter My Heart
Trapped by Fate on Reckless Roads
Thunderstruck

5-Star Reviews for the stories of the NTNT MC series

This is the Route of Twisted Pain

"This is the Route of Twisted Pain is an exhilarating, gripping romance novel contrived of incredible world building, complex yet relatable characters, and a unique, captivating plot.

Gifted storyteller MariaLisa deMora beautifully balances exciting suspense, fast action, intriguing secrets with delicious, blazing hot romance scenes.

Readers will be up all night with this riveting page-turner."

~ NY Literary Magazine

I am completely tickled in my fancy for TWISTED!

First off, let me state that there was one thing I didn't like about this book and that is the LAST PAGE! I hated for it to end. I dearly loved this book and its characters as well as their setting.

~Colleen M.

Gripping tale

Twisted and Penny fit together beautifully. The book covers so much more than just their love story. Great introduction to the Incoherent MC. The tale is gripping and gritty. The journey is full of twists and turns that keep you on the edge of your seat. I couldn't put it down. Cannot wait for the next one.

~Lillmil

Twisted is one of the most original and interesting characters I have read in a long time. Marialisa's character building is setting a high bar for her to follow, she will hopefully continue with Po'Boy's story. The Route of Twisted Pain was pure brilliance, and I highly recommend this read.
~Penny T.

This book obsessed me!
This may be the best book I read all year.
These people...they're not characters, they're real... have stuck in my head from the day I met them.
MariaLisa deMora can throw words down that'll Twist (hehe) your insides up till you can't breathe for waiting to hear what's next!
I'm working my way through her other 'families' and yup...she really is that good.
~DeLane

Treading the Traitor's Path: Out Bad

"Treading the Traitor's Path: Out Bad is a solidly engrossing, well-written novel by a talented author.
MariaLisa deMora delivers a thrilling ride filled with exciting suspense, deliciously explicit, vivid sex scenes, and gritty, fast-paced action. Her characters are smart, complex, and strong with sharp edges. The settings meticulously detailed.
Fans of Motorcycle Club romance stories will not want to miss this second installment in deMora's exciting series."
~ NY Literary Magazine

Book Hangover

What an amazing read! DeMora does not simply wrote a book, she pulls you into a different world. When you read her work, you are very much surrounded by the characters and setting. Prepare for a book hangover because once you finish the book, you will still be stuck with Po Boy.
~KW

More More More

THIS WAS AMAZING. Highly recommend for a good story line, interesting characters. I just wish there was more more more.
~Laura

Loved This Book!

What did I just read?! Is my kindle still working? I'm pretty sure it combusted into flames while reading this story. RED HOT READ for 2017. Not what I was expecting at all! I tend to stay away from ménage a trois, because for me it's hard to say there's any kind of conflict except for jealousy, and the ending kind of leaves things unresolved and unrealistic. NOT THIS BOOK! The best one out there guaranteed.
~Linda A

So Freaking Good

...seriously this series is just WTF so freaking good. Dark, Twisted, harsh, painful and raw. Po'Boy lives for his club, his brothers and his family, there is nothing he wouldn't do for them.
~Fay

The author delivers a 5-STAR READ

I live and breathe for books like this! Fabulously Naughty!...Wickedly Hot! This is my first book by MariaLisa deMora and it will not be my last. MariaLisa delivered a 5 STAR READ! The plot is filled with action, suspense, romance and tons of hot scenes.

~Jenny F

~~~~~
~~~~~

Alace Sweets, a dark romantic suspense standalone

A dark thriller, this book is not a light read. Filled with edge-of-your-seat suspense, this intense story commands the reader's attention as it drives towards the explosive ending. Alace Sweets is a vigilante serial killer, with everything that implies and is sure to trip all your triggers. Be ready.

At seventeen, Alace Sweets turned a corner in her life, taking the wrong shortcut home from school.

Resisting the harsh knowledge her attackers will never be made to pay for their actions, Alace takes a stand. Justice must be served, and if fate's scales are out of balance, she's determined to set things right as best she can.

When the laws of men fail, the rules of Alace prevail.

5-Star Reviews for Alace Sweets

"Whatever deep dark trench [deMora] pulled a character like Alace from should be revisited again and often."
~Confessions of a Serial Reader

"deMora has a superb story-line and exceptional character development. All of her characters have such depth that will intrigue the reader..."
~Turning Another Page

"Hot, sweet, dark thriller."
~Beth D

"It will keep you on the edge of your seat and give you chills."
~Escape Reality Book Blog

"Disturbing, haunting, sickly; yet hot, sexy and heart racing!"
~Amanda L

"From the first page [deMora] pulls you into the world she has created and you do not even try to escape..."
~Little Shop of Readers Blog

"A must read for all those dark, gritty romance fans out there."
~Sweet & Spicy Reads

"You will find yourself so drawn into the story that the outside world is blocked out and your locking the doors and turning on all the lights."
~Danena F

"Don't judge me for bonding with a vigilante serial killer, she's more than what she does."
~iScream Books

"Thrilling...chilling...full of suspense, nail biting edge of your seat excitement."
~Tracey H

"Every time MariaLisa deMora picks up her pen (or opens her computer), she creates characters you want to believe in."
~Gail S

"Intriguing dark storyline, beautiful love story and nail-biting conclusion, what more could a reader ask for?"
~Manda M

"This book takes you a dark and twisted ride that is gripping..."
~Renee Entress' Blog

"This book is dark and gritty and I literally had to take a day off from reading it because it's that intense."
~My Girlfriend's Couch

"This is my favourite book so far from this author ... I recommend this book if you enjoy dark romantic thrillers."
~Cheekypee Reads and Reviews

"There's not enough stars to give this book and 5 just doesn't really do it justice!"
~DeLane C

"I couldn't put this book down from page one! Tried to stop & go to bed but couldn't sleep thinking about Alace and got up & finished the book."
~Debbie M

“MariaLisa DeMora, wordsmith that she is, made this a story of the enlightenment of a woman and finding love in a life where she has had none.”
~Kat W

~~~~~
~~~~~

Hard Focus, a criminal thriller standalone

This is an intense page-turner, a gut-punch twist-filled story about a woman who has confidence in herself, believes she's a good judge of character, and has filled her life with people she can trust. She's right, but she's also very, very wrong. Readers will have a time of it trying to decide who to watch closest.

Where do you place your trust when your own instincts betray you?

Connie Rowe is a receptionist at a respected legal firm. She's a little bit sassy, a lotta bit happy, has good friends, and is adored by her neighbors.

Life is good.

She's got a boyfriend she enjoys spending time with. He can be a little intense, but he's got a lot going on in his own life, sorting out his young daughter and nightmare of an ex.

Life is grand.

"Trust your gut." That's what Connie's police officer father told her often, training his daughter to believe in herself through the years.

But … what happens when you can't? When your intuition lies?

What happens when things come into Hard Focus?

5-Star Reviews for Hard Focus

"Hard Focus is one very well-written tale. 5 stars is not enough for me."
~Tabitha

"What a powerful story. [deMora] kept me invested from the first word to the last."
~Jesse R

"[deMora] has a certain magical touch to writing her characters, that they become either your nemesis, your best friend, or your love interest. That is certainly portrayed in this spin around. Loved it, loved it, loved it."
~Sandy K

"I strongly recommend this book for both entertainment and to broaden your knowledge of certain laws that must be revisited."
~Words Turn Me On

"An intense page turner. Once you start, you can't put the book down."
~Tracey H

"A beautifully written, powerful read that I can't rate highly enough. This story will stay with me always."
~Gayle

"This book had twists I didn't see coming. Loved it!"
~Lori R

"Wow! I am in awe of deMora's skill in crafting this story."
~Kat W

"I keep sayin that there just aren't enough stars to give to some of Marialisa deMora's books...this one is no different!"
~DeLane

"Where do I start with this one...I read this in 3 1/2 hours uninterrupted, I absolutely could NOT put it down. Very deep, keeps you guessing, what's gonna happen next, kind of book. I love how strong her characters are, especially the females!"
~Wendy I

"Sometimes I feel like MariaLisa deMora is the one I should be watching out for. I started reading her books because I'm addicted to MC Romance, but then she decides to change things up and I just follow her wherever she leads me like a Pied Piper. I never know what to expect, and sometimes I'm afraid to find out, but it's always an adventure."
~Rosa for iScream Books Blog

"A plot full of twists and turns, a story that's not quite what it seems, strong characterization, jaw dropping revelations... what more do you need from a book?"
~Manda M

"This book kept me turning the pages wondering what was going to happen. I am usually pretty good at guessing twists but not with this book. She totally surprised me and brought me out of my funk. 5 stars."
~Glenna M

"What an amazing story! Filled with a smidge of suspense, a dash of action and a heap of realism of our country's laws and how their vague application to victims can adversely affect its citizens and the people in their lives."
~Naughty Mom Story Time

ADDITIONAL SERIES AND BOOKS

Please note that books in a series frequently feature characters from additional books within that series. If series books are read out of order, readers will twig to spoilers for the other books, so going back to read the skipped titles won't have the same angsty reveals.

Rebel Wayfarers MC series:

Mica, #1
A Sweet & Merry Christmas, #1.5
Slate, #2
Bear, #3
Jase, #4
Gunny, #5
Mason, #6
Hoss, #7
Harddrive Holidays, #7.5
Duck, #8
Biker Chick Campout, #8.5
Watcher, #9
A Kiss to Keep You, #9.25
Gun Totin' Annie, #9.5
Secret Santa, #9.75
Bones, #10
Gunny's Pups, #10.25
Never Settle, #10.5
Not Even A Mouse, #10.75
Fury, #11
Christmas Doings, #11.25
Gypsy's Lady, #11.5
Cassie, #12
Road Runner's Ride, #12.5

Occupy Yourself band series:

Born Into Trouble, #1
Grace In Motion, #2 (TBD)
What They Say, #3 (TBD)

Neither This, Nor That MC series:

This Is the Route Of Twisted Pain, #1
Treading the Traitor's Path: Out Bad, #2
Shelter My Heart, #3
Trapped by Fate on Reckless Roads, #4
Thunderstruck, #5

Rebel Wayfarers & Incoherent MC (NTNT) crossover stories:

Going Down Easy
No Man's Land

Mayhan Bucklers MC series:

Most Rikki-Tik, #1
Mad Minute, #2
Pucker Factor, #3
Boocoo Dinky Dau, #4 (TBD)

Borderline Freaks MC series:

Service and Sacrifice, #1
More Than Enough, #2
Lack of In-between, #3
See You in Valhalla, #4